THE SECRET LIFE OF
MARY ANNE SPIER

**Other books by
Ann M. Martin**

Leo the Magnificat
Rachel Parker, Kindergarten Show-off
Eleven Kids, One Summer
Ma and Pa Dracula
Yours Turly, Shirley
Ten Kids, No Pets
Slam Book
Just a Summer Romance
Missing Since Monday
With You and Without You
Me and Katie (the Pest)
Stage Fright
Inside Out
Bummer Summer

THE KIDS IN MS. COLMAN'S CLASS series
BABY-SITTERS LITTLE SISTER series
THE BABY-SITTERS CLUB mysteries
THE BABY-SITTERS CLUB series
CALIFORNIA DIARIES series

THE SECRET LIFE OF
MARY ANNE SPIER

Ann M. Martin

AN
APPLE
PAPERBACK

SCHOLASTIC INC.
New York Toronto London Auckland Sydney

Cover art by Hodges Soileau

ISBN 0-590-05992-0

12 11 10 9 8 7 6 5 4 3 2 1   7 8 9/9 0 1 2/0

Printed in the U.S.A.   40

First Scholastic printing, December 1997

*The author gratefully acknowledges
Suzanne Weyn
for her help in
preparing this manuscript.*

CHAPTER 1

Click. As I placed Dad's credit card on the counter at the BookCenter in the Washington Mall, the plastic made the softest sound. It's amazing how a little thing like the click of a credit card can send thrills through you.

Glancing at my friend Kristy Thomas, I grinned. "I've never done this before," I whispered with a shiver of excitement.

"Really?" Kristy raised an eyebrow. "It's no big deal."

Maybe it's not to her. Her stepdad, Watson Brewer, is a millionaire, after all. But my father had never before allowed me to use his credit card. It made me feel so incredibly grown-up, so sophisticated, to be doing my Christmas shopping with plastic this year.

Click, again — the sound of the saleswoman picking up the card. She read it and then turned to me. "Do you have any identification?" she asked.

"Sure." I fished through my wallet for my Stoneybrook Middle School student identification card and handed it to her. The woman studied it intently. Maybe it was my imagination, but she seemed unsure that the picture on the card was of me.

"I had long hair when that picture was taken," I explained. "But I had it cut shorter. You can tell it's me, though. Mary Anne Spier. See? The same name as on the credit card. Well, not the exact same name. My dad is Richard Spier, of course, but the last name matches."

The woman looked up and smiled as she handed the I.D. card back to me. "Yes, it's you, all right. Sorry, but I have to check."

"No problem," I assured her. "I guess you can't be too careful, especially now, around the holidays."

The woman nodded as she processed my sale. I'd bought my stepmom, Sharon, a thick book called *Veggies Rule.* She's a vegetarian and eats only healthy foods. The book wasn't only a cookbook; it also had great art and amusing stories about vegetables. "She'll like this, don't you think?" I asked Kristy.

"When you put it together with the automatic bread maker you bought her, it makes an awesome gift," Kristy replied. "It might be a little *too* awesome."

The woman returned Dad's card and handed

me the book in a bag. I thanked her and turned to Kristy. "What do you mean?"

"One or the other would have been enough, don't you think?"

"Oh, but Sharon's so great and she's had such a hard year with Dawn moving away and all," I said, defending my spending. Dawn Schafer, my stepsister, is Sharon's daughter. This year she decided to move back to California to live with her father, brother, and her father's new wife.

Dawn's decision to move took us all by surprise. She had seemed happy living with Dad, Sharon, and me. For awhile, I was so upset that I didn't notice how sad it was making Sharon.

No matter how much Dawn tried to explain that she wasn't moving because of us — she simply missed the West Coast — it hurt. We all miss her.

"I know you're softhearted and generous," Kristy told me. "I admire that. But didn't your father give you a limit on what you could spend?"

"Sort of."

"What does that mean?" Kristy is a get-to-the-point person and has no patience for vague answers. But sometimes the truth isn't so clear-cut.

"He said not to spend more than I could afford to pay back," I explained.

3

"Well? How much is that?"

"It depends."

Kristy blew out a puff of air and her brown bangs flew up. She didn't have to say anything. I knew she was thinking, *Can't you be more specific than that?* Kristy and I have been close friends since we were little.

"I can't be exactly sure!" I cried, throwing my arms out. (Which caused all the shopping bags I had slung on my arms to slide back and hit me on the sides.) "I don't know the number of baby-sitting jobs I'm going to be able to take between now and Christmas. I can't tell how many will come in or who else will want them. It's been so busy, though. I think we'll all do well."

I was talking about the Baby-sitters Club, otherwise known as the BSC. It's a club Kristy founded. Clients call one number and reach several qualified baby-sitters at once. (I'll tell you more details later.) Ever since Thanksgiving, business had been outrageously busy. We could hardly handle the number of clients who called. So, even though I couldn't predict *exactly* the amount of money I'd earn, I was sure it would be plenty.

We left the bookstore and were in the mall again. "Why don't we go to Stuff 'N Nonsense next?" Kristy suggested. "Dawn likes the earrings they sell there."

"Okay," I agreed. We headed toward Stuff 'N Nonsense, a funky store with lots of trendy jewelry. I'd shopped for my friends yesterday, so today I only had family left to shop for, and then I'd be done.

I couldn't believe how crowded the mall was. People knocked into us and didn't even realize it.

We passed through the center court on the first floor. The fountain that usually spurts pink water had been turned off and a huge Christmas tree stood in front of it. Beside it, some mall workers were busily hammering a platform into place. Soon a Santa would sit on the platform, taking gift orders from the excited kids who would line up to meet him. (Other years, Lear's department store had run a North Pole Village featuring Santa. This year, though, the mall was running what it called Winter World.)

"Look at that," said Kristy, pointing to a sign propped up against the half-built platform. It read: HOLIDAY HELP WANTED. APPLY AT SPECIAL EVENTS OFFICE. "Only two weeks until Christmas, and they're still hiring extra help?" she asked.

"Hanukkah comes after Christmas this year, and so does Kwanzaa," I pointed out, "so there's really *more* than two weeks until gift-buying ends."

"That's true," Kristy replied. "Do people exchange Kwanzaa gifts?"

"I don't think it's in the actual tradition of Kwanzaa, but sometimes people do give gifts anyway," I said, trying to remember what I'd learned in school, and from my friend Jessi Ramsey. "And even if they're not buying gifts, they still buy new tablecloths and candles and baskets — things like that."

For a moment we stood and watched the workers assemble the platform. "I wonder what it's like to be a mall Santa," Kristy said. "Do you think it's fun or totally weird?"

I shrugged. "I don't know. Embarrassing, maybe. What do you do when people you know come along?"

"Duck behind an elf," Kristy said.

I started laughing, thinking how ridiculous that would look. "I don't think that would do Santa much good. He's too fat to fit behind an elf."

"You're right. I guess he'd have to find a fat elf."

Still laughing, we continued on to Stuff 'N Nonsense. Kristy had been right. They had earrings I was sure Dawn would love. After looking at almost *every* pair in the store, I spotted metallic linked hoops in red, silver, and blue. They were totally Dawn. "She has two holes in each ear so I'll have to buy two pairs," I said.

"Isn't that going overboard?" Kristy asked.

"No, she'll wear them all together," I said, confident that I knew Dawn's taste. "And look at this," I added, reading the piece of cardboard they were attached to. "They're made from recycled aluminum cans."

"She'll *love* that," Kristy agreed. Dawn is very committed to the environment, especially when it comes to recycling.

"There's a matching necklace!" I cried as I crossed the store to it.

"I think the earrings are enough," said Kristy.

"Please! Dawn will love this. I *have* to buy it for her."

"If you say so."

I frowned at her. "Aren't you excited about seeing Dawn?" I asked. I put the earrings and necklace on the counter and handed the salesclerk the credit card. "She and Jeff are arriving this coming Monday." (Jeff is my younger stepbrother.)

"Sure I want to see Dawn," Kristy replied.

"Well, me too. I want to get her something really nice to let her know how happy I am to see her." The salesclerk handed me my bag. "Where do you want to go next?" I asked.

Kristy checked her watch. "We better head to

Claudia's house. We have a meeting in forty-five minutes. Can you imagine what would happen if I was late?"

I laughed and rolled my eyes in pretend horror. "It would be the end of the world!"

CHAPTER 2

The reason I'd said it would be the end of the world was because Kristy has never been late for a BSC meeting without having an airtight excuse. And she *insists* that everyone else be on time too. If you're late, she stares at you in a glowering way that makes you want to disappear. We call this the Look. We avoid it at all cost.

That day, Kristy and I came extremely close to being late. The bus from the mall was caught in horrible, crawling holiday traffic. Two women sitting in front of us debated if it was because there was construction on the Connecticut Turnpike, or if it was simply because holiday shopping was heavier than usual this year.

I had no clue. I only knew Kristy was tense. Her hands were clenched into fists. She chewed her lower lip. I could almost read her mind. If she was late she'd have to endure endless teasing. Then everyone else would think that if she was late, *they* could be late sometimes too. Chaos would overtake the club. No one would want us anymore. The club would fall apart completely.

I didn't think any of this would happen, of course. But it was the kind of thing Kristy worried about. You see, she's the club president. After she came up with the idea for the BSC, she asked me and another friend, Claudia Kishi, if we wanted to form the club, which is really a baby-sitting business. We would all be available in Claudia's room (she has a private phone line) between five-thirty and six on Mondays, Wednesdays, and Fridays to take calls from clients. We recruited Claudia's friend, Stacey McGill, to join us and we placed flyers and posters around town.

We were an instant success. Business grew so busy that when I met Dawn I asked her to join. (Before we were stepsisters, we were friends.) The BSC has been a huge part of my life — of all our lives — ever since.

But, of course, Kristy wasn't thinking about the past as the bus crawled at a snail's pace through downtown Stoneybrook. Instead, she was thinking about the present — the meeting that was going to start any minute.

We raced off the bus at 5:25 and soon were charging down Bradford Court. Mushy patches of slush flew out from under our feet, splattering our shopping bags. We didn't care.

Kristy is very athletic and soon outdistanced me by a half block. When I arrived, panting, at Claudia's doorstep, my heart hammering, Kristy was just standing in front of the door, looking stricken. "What's the matter?" I said, puffing.

"What if I'm late?" she asked.

I grabbed her wrist and pushed open the door. (Mrs. Kishi leaves it open on club days.) "Come on and find out," I said, half dragging her up the stairs.

When we stepped into Claudia's room, all the regular club members were there. "Rats!" cried Abby Stevenson, swinging back her dark curls. "It's five-thirty on the dot. We were hoping you'd be late."

Kristy grinned at the digital clock on Claudia's dresser. Then she scowled. "Why were you hoping we'd be late?"

"So we could do this," Stacey answered. She furrowed her brow and glared at Kristy. At the same time, so did Abby, Claudia, Jessi Ramsey, and Mallory Pike, each giving Kristy her own version of the Look.

I burst out laughing. Even Kristy — who takes this matter deadly seriously — smiled.

The phone rang and the meeting started. Claudia was closest to the phone, so she grabbed it. "Hello, Baby-sitters Club." It was Dr. Johanssen. She needed someone to sit for Charlotte the next day, Saturday afternoon. "I'll call you right back," Claudia told her.

That's how we always operate. We take the information about the job, then hang up. As club secretary, it's my job to check the club record book and see who's available. Everyone's schedule is in the book — not only their baby-sitting jobs but their doctor appointments, after-school activities, vacations, everything. I saw that Stacey was free, and I know she loves Charlotte Johanssen, so I offered her the job first. "Absolutely," she replied. "I'll be there."

Claudia called Dr. Johanssen back and reported that Stacey would be coming.

From my usual spot on Claudia's bed, I gazed around the room and thought of all the cool gifts I'd gotten my friends. I couldn't wait to see their faces when they received them.

"Notebook!" Kristy said, holding up a spiral notebook. "Who wants it first?"

"Not me," Claudia said, waving it away. The club notebook is where we write about our baby-sitting jobs. Kristy insists we do it because it's good to know which kids are difficult, or scared of certain things, or have allergies, or whatever else. If a sitter goes to a

12

new job, she can refer to the book and instantly know what to expect.

Most of us don't like to be bothered with the notebook, especially Claudia, who's a terrible speller and hates writing in general. In fact, she has such a difficult time with schoolwork that she was switched back to the seventh grade for awhile. She's returned to eighth grade now, but school is still a struggle. To make matters worse, her older sister, Janine, is an actual genius. But I think Mr. and Mrs. Kishi have given up comparing the girls.

For Christmas I found the best art set for Claudia, complete with pastels, oils, watercolors, and markers. I knew she'd love it. Art is Claudia's passion. There, no one can come close to her. She is *so* talented.

Claudia is also beautiful, with long black hair and almond eyes (she's Japanese-American). She looks great in the unique outfits she creates for herself with beads, feathers, fabric paint, and anything else that pops into her always-creative mind.

Since we meet in Claudia's room and use her phone, she's the club's vice-president. She's also in charge of hospitality. It's a natural job for Claudia, because all she has to do is pull bags of junk food out from under her bed, behind pillows, or the back of her closet. She *loves* junk food but has to hide it (like she hides her Nancy Drew books) since her parents don't approve.

"I'll write in the notebook!" Mallory volunteered. She's the only one of us who really enjoys writing in it because she wants to be a writer. Actually, her goal is to be an author-illustrator of children's books.

Mallory says she never wants her picture to appear on the dust jacket of a book she writes because she doesn't like her looks, especially her nose. She has reddish-brown hair, glasses, and braces (the clear kind). Maybe she's not gorgeous (like Claudia or Stacey), but I think she's cute. Besides, she's only eleven. Her looks might change a lot in the next few years.

"Jessi and I sat for my brothers and sisters yesterday," Mallory reported as she opened up the notebook. "What a zoo!" This was no big surprise. Mal's the oldest of *eight* kids. She'd have plenty of pictures to put into the big photo album I'd bought her for Christmas.

Jessi looked over Mallory's shoulder and giggled at what Mallory was writing. "When Nicky got stuck in the basket, it was hard not to laugh," she said to Mallory, who is her best friend.

Like Mallory, Jessi is eleven. They're our two junior officers. They can only sit in the daytime (unless they're sitting for their own siblings).

14

But that's okay. It frees the rest of us, who are all thirteen, to take night jobs.

I was sure Jessi would love the tickets I'd bought her at the Ticket Booth at the mall. They were for a Saturday matinee of *The Nutcracker* being performed in Stamford, the nearest city to Stoneybrook. (I'd already marked Jessi unavailable for that day in the record book.) I knew she'd be thrilled because Jessi is a talented ballerina who has appeared in several professional productions. She studies at a dance school in Stamford.

You can tell Jessi is a dancer simply by looking at her. She's tall and slim with long legs and graceful posture. She even wears her black hair the way dancers often do, pulled off her face.

Like Mallory, Jessi's the oldest kid in her family. Her sister, Becca, is eight, and her baby brother, Squirt, is nearly two. (His real name is John Philip, Jr.) Their aunt Cecelia lives with them and takes care of Squirt while Jessi's parents are at work. The Ramseys moved to Stoneybrook because Mr. Ramsey was transferred here by his company. The Ramseys are African-American, so some people in mostly white Stoneybrook gave them a hard time at first, but things are better now.

"I'm collecting dues today since we were too busy to do it on Monday," Stacey announced to

15

a general chorus of groans. Monday is usually dues day. But the phone didn't stop ringing all day Monday *or* Wednesday. So she never had the chance to collect. Stacey jiggled the few remaining coins in the manila envelope where she keeps the BSC's money. "Come on, we're nearly broke after last week's pizza party," she announced. "Open your wallets, kiddies. You didn't actually think you'd get away without paying this week, did you?"

Stacey's the treasurer because she's our math whiz, so she has to perform this very unpopular job. No one wants to fork over, but we know we have to. The money pays for things we need. For instance we pay part of Claudia's phone bill. And we pay Kristy's brother Charlie to drive Kristy and Abby to meetings since they live on the other side of town.

We also use dues money to restock Kid-Kits. Each of us has her own box full of toys, coloring books, art supplies — all sorts of fun stuff. We don't bring them on every job, but they often come in handy if a kid is sick or if he or she is a new client.

If there's any money left over, we do something fun, such as hold a pizza party like we did last week.

Stacey passed the envelope around, not listening to our complaints. I smiled to myself, thinking of the earmuffs that I'd bought as part of her Christmas gift. I was going to tell her I'd bought them for her so she wouldn't have to listen to us grumble anymore.

Of course, there was more to the gift than earmuffs. I'd bought her a cheetah-print set: a hat, leather-trimmed gloves, and a scarf. I was *pretty* sure she'd like it but not positive. I bought it because I know she likes clothing. I was worried, though. Stacey's sense of style is much more sophisticated than mine. That's probably because she grew up in New York City. And in a way, she still lives there part-time. Her parents are divorced and her dad has an apartment in the city. She stays with him on a lot of weekends.

As I mentioned, Stacey is beautiful, with giant blue eyes and shoulder-length blonde, wavy hair. Despite being gifted with brains and beauty, her life isn't perfect. One big problem is her diabetes. That's a serious condition in which the levels of sugar in her bloodstream can become dangerously high. To keep those sugar levels under control, she has to give herself injections of insulin daily and keep to a strict diet.

Stacey doesn't let this get her down, though. (At least most of the time she doesn't.) She does what she has to do and pretty much leads a normal life.

"Oh, please, Mrs. Scrooge, don't take my last

dime," Abby joked, pretending to cower as Stacey presented the dues envelope to her. "Tiny Tim needs this coin."

"Cough it up, Abby Cratchit," Stacey said.

Everyone laughed. But then, Abby often keeps us laughing — and she's always a little offbeat. She claims her oddball sense of humor comes from living on Long Island, outside of New York City. "Everybody there is like me," she claims. I simply can't believe that's true, though. Abby is one of a kind.

Well . . . not *entirely* one of a kind. Abby has a twin sister, Anna. Their father was killed in a car accident when they were nine. So it's just the girls and their mother, who works in publishing in New York. Kristy was the first of us to meet Abby, when the Stevensons recently moved in only one house away from Watson's mansion. She thought Abby might be a good replacement for Dawn, and she's been a member ever since.

Since Abby's our newest member, she was the hardest for me to pick a gift for. But I know she likes sports, so finally I bought Kristy and Abby the same gift — a catcher's mitt. Logan (my boyfriend) told me it was a terrific one. (It had better be, for the price I paid.)

Speaking of Logan, I should tell you that he's adorable, wonderful, has sandy-colored hair and a smooth southern accent (he grew up in

Kentucky). He's on the football team, and he's also an associate member of the BSC. (Doesn't he sound perfect? He is. Most of the time, anyway.) Being an associate member means that we call him when we have more work than we can handle but he doesn't attend meetings regularly.

Our other associate member is Shannon Kilbourne, who lives near Kristy and Abby. Originally, we wanted *her* to take Dawn's place. But that didn't work out. Shannon attends a private school, Stoneybrook Day, and she was already committed to after-school activities. She can still fill in when we really need her, though.

The phone rang again. This time it was Mrs. Rodowsky, who needed a sitter for Archie, Jackie, and Shea for the next afternoon. Claudia took that job.

Almost as soon as Claudia hung up, the phone rang a third time. It was Mrs. DeWitt wanting a sitter for her gang of kids and step-kids, also for the next afternoon. "Is something special going on tomorrow?" asked Kristy, who'd taken the call. She listened, nodding for awhile. "That's terrible," she said seriously. "Okay. We'll call you back."

"What's terrible?" Jessi asked, looking up from the club notebook.

Kristy told us what Mrs. DeWitt had told her. Dr. Johanssen had called together a group of volunteers to discuss the Toys for Kids program. In previous years, the program was run by the hospital where Dr. Johanssen works. It provided gifts for sick kids who'd have to spend the holidays there. Due to budget cuts, the program wasn't being sponsored this year.

"I wonder if there's a way we could help?" Kristy said as she sat forward in her chair.

I was looking in the record book for a sitter for the seven Barrett-DeWitts. (Two sitters, actually. We always send two for more than four kids.) I glanced at Kristy and could almost hear the wheels in her brain turning. She was working on the Toys for Kids situation.

Kristy is one of the most remarkable people I know. Although, like me, she's petite in size, she has a big personality. She's a can-do person who gets a *lot* done. She runs the club like a pro. She also coaches a kids' softball team called Kristy's Krushers.

Kristy's not into clothes or her looks. Mostly she wears jeans or sweats, and pulls her shoulder-length brown hair back into a ponytail. But she always makes an impression on people. Maybe it's because she's so direct and sincere.

Even though, as I mentioned, her stepdad's a millionaire, Kristy hasn't always had things easy. Her birth father abandoned the family soon after her little brother, David Michael, was born. Her mother had to raise and support four kids on her own. (Kristy also has two older brothers, Sam and Charlie.) It was a real struggle. Eventually, though, Mrs. Thomas met Watson and they married, *and* she got a huge promotion at her job. Now Kristy and her brothers live in Watson's mansion. Karen and Andrew, her two younger step-siblings, live there every other month. And Watson and Kristy's mom adopted a baby girl from Vietnam, Emily Michelle, who is two and a half. Kristy's grandmother, Nannie, has come to live with them. All these people, along with assorted pets, make a very full house.

And, speaking of people with full houses — I assigned the Barrett-DeWitt job to Abby and Jessi.

"I know!" Kristy said. "The BSC will run a fund-raiser to help Toys for Kids."

"Great! What will we do?" Mallory asked.

Kristy frowned. "I'm still working on that part."

CHAPTER 3

I was filled with Christmas spirit when I returned home from our meeting that afternoon. My Christmas shopping was finished. I was pleased with my purchases. I'd found just the right gift for each person. And now I could look forward to wrapping, which I enjoy.

The fireplace in the living room of our old farmhouse (built in 1774!) blazed. In the corner stood the huge Christmas tree Dad and I had chopped down ourselves at a tree farm the weekend before. Sharon and I had put twinkly lights on the tree and wrapped it in the gold-beaded garlands we'd taken from the attic. We were leaving the rest of the decorations for when Jeff and Dawn arrived.

Dad sat on the couch by the fireplace, paging through a jewelry catalog. (I guess he was looking for Sharon's gift.) "Whoa!" he said with a wary laugh as I dragged my shopping bags into the room. "More gifts? I thought you finished yesterday."

"No, but now I'm done," I said, settling the bags around my feet.

Dad frowned at the bags. "It looks like you were very . . . generous."

I shrugged. "I suppose."

"You put all this on my card?" he asked.

Digging out my wallet from my purse, I handed the card back to him. "Yes, but I'm paying you back. Remember?"

"With interest?" he asked.

Now it was my turn to look disturbed. I didn't like the sound of this. "What do you mean?"

Putting down his catalog, Dad sat forward. "If a person doesn't pay his credit card bill in full, then the card company charges a percentage of the total outstanding balance until it's completely paid off. It can really add up."

"Do you mean that the things I bought can wind up costing me more than I paid for them?"

Dad nodded. "A lot more."

I thought for a moment, then smiled. "Well, don't worry. I'll be able to pay you as soon as the bill comes in. So interest is of no *interest* to me."

"Very funny," he said dryly, looking relieved.

I sniffed the air. Something wonderful was cooking. "Hungry?" he asked. "I made stew."

"Yes!" I cried. I like Dad's cooking so much better than Sharon's. She's not a bad cook, she just likes to eat the weirdest stuff. It was a major problem when our families blended. Sharon and Dawn were grossed out by all the meat and packaged foods Dad and I eat. Dad and I were equally disturbed by seaweed, tofu, miso, sprouts, and all that healthy stuff they like. One tiny benefit of Dawn's leaving is that now Dad and I rule the kitchen. "Did you make it with beef or tofu?" I asked, concerned that the answer might be tofu. (Dad tries to be fair to Sharon.)

"Both," he replied, getting up from the couch.

Okay, I thought, *fair is fair*. I'd pick out the tofu. Sharon would pick out the beef. Dad would eat both, and we'd all eat the vegetables.

At dinner, Sharon, who is usually pretty disorganized, was really beside herself. She put some butter in the microwave to soften it, and it melted into a yellow puddle. She forgot about the instant biscuits she'd stuck in the oven. Then the smoke detector went off.

"Where's my fork?" she asked just as she was about to eat.

"Right there," Dad told her, pointing to the breast pocket of her blazer.

24

She took the fork out and laughed. "Oh, gosh. I must have put it there when the phone rang." She set the fork on the table. "I guess I'm just so excited about Dawn and Jeff coming that I can't think of anything else."

"I found the best gift for Dawn," I told her.

She lifted her hand to silence me. "Don't tell me," she said. "I like to be surprised by everyone's gifts."

After dinner I helped clean up and then brought the rest of my shopping bags upstairs. I put them in Dawn's room, where I'd left the others. Popping a disc of holiday music into Dawn's CD player, I settled in for an evening of wrapping.

I'd bought the most beautiful wrapping paper at the mall. My favorite had a cream background with old-fashioned Santas all over it. I bought another with penguins in Santa suits skiing down a hill. And another one had golden stars on a deep blue background. I'd probably gone overboard on buying ribbon — metallic fuchsia, gold, bright green, one extra-wide roll with a calico print — but who can resist ribbon? I can't.

As I wrapped, I felt overwhelmed with happiness. It was one of those moods you can't exactly explain. But why shouldn't I be happy? I adore the holidays. I have a happy family, good friends, and Dawn was coming home. And, thanks to Dad's credit card, I'd be able to show all the important people in my life how much they mean to me.

I spent hours wrapping, enjoying every bow. With each package, I grew more creative, expanding the bows with extra ribbon, combining papers and ribbons. What fun!

The results were beautiful. By eleven o'clock, I sat amid a sea of gorgeously wrapped packages. I pictured how awesome they'd look sitting under the tree.

Then I thought: Why wait? Why not put them under the tree now? Dawn and Jeff would feel so festive when they arrived and saw packages already under the tree.

After several trips up and down the stairs I'd finally placed all my packages around the tree. "Wow!" Sharon said as I put the last ones into place. "Look at all those gifts! Did you win the lottery this year?"

I saw what she meant. The presents made a small mountain around the tree. I couldn't believe it. Why did it seem like more than other years? I'd bought gifts for all the same people.

I realized that the boxes were all on the large side. And this year I'd bought some people more than one gift. Even Dawn's small jewelry boxes looked large since I'd stacked the three of them on top of one another and tied them together with gold ribbon.

"Did you save *all* your baby-sitting money this year?" Sharon asked, circling the tree. "How did you ever afford this?"

"I saved for the last two months," I told her. "And since I used Dad's credit card, I can use the money I make in the next thirty days. I was figuring I actually have six weeks because he doesn't have to pay the bill right away."

"Two weeks," Sharon said.

"What?"

"That bill comes in at the end of the month," she told me. "And your dad always pays right away. So you can use the money you earn in the next *two* weeks. You don't have six weeks." She must have noticed my horrified expression. "I'm sure your dad will give you extra time if you can't pay," she added.

Dad came into the room. "Sure, with interest," he said.

"You'd charge her interest?" Sharon gasped.

"Sure I would. Why should I pay the interest on her gifts? I'd wind up buying my own gift," he replied sensibly.

"Don't you think that's a little harsh?" Sharon objected.

"No. What's harsh about it? If Mary Anne is responsible enough to use a credit card, then she has to be held responsible for everything that goes with it. It doesn't matter, though, because she says she has the money. Right?"

Sharon looked at me but didn't mention that I'd thought I had six weeks to earn the money I didn't yet have. I was grateful. I'd enjoyed using the card and wanted to be able to use it again. Besides, I'd have the money.

At least I thought I would.

But I was suddenly uneasy. It wasn't as though I'd done an exact mathematical tally. I'd estimated what I thought I had, what I thought I'd make, and what I thought I was spending — very roughly.

Maybe it was time to be exact.

Sharon took her camera from the mantel. "The tree looks so lovely with the gifts around it. I have to take a picture." She began snapping.

"Want some hot cider, Mary Anne?" Dad offered. "I'm heating it."

"No thanks," I replied absently. "I have something I need to do right now."

"Please don't tell me you're wrapping *more* gifts," Dad teased.

I shot him a quick smile. "No, something else." I ran upstairs and searched through the debris I'd left on Dawn's floor — the old bags, the crumpled tissue paper, the empty ribbon spools, and scattered wrapping-paper clippings. From under it all I pulled a small brown bag in which I'd been stuffing the receipts of my purchases in case anything needed to be returned.

Sitting cross-legged on Dawn's bed, I dumped out the receipts. With the pen I'd been using to write out gift tags, I transferred prices from the receipts onto the empty bag. My heartbeat quickened as I kept adding. The list seemed almost endless. As I reached the bottom of the bag I had to write smaller and smaller to fit everything on.

The first time I added the numbers, I scratched out my answer. It had to be wrong. I could not possibly have spent that much money. Could I have? No! I added again and discovered that, as I thought, I had been mistaken. I'd actually spent five dollars *more* than the first number I'd reached.

The next two times I added I came up with the same astronomical figure — three times the amount of money I had saved.

Three times!

I didn't understand how this could have happened. At the mall, it just hadn't seemed as if I was spending that much money. Maybe it was the credit card. When you don't actually see the money leaving your hand it doesn't seem as though you're spending it.

What should I do? What *could* I do? The gifts were already wrapped and under the tree. I couldn't take them back. Well, I supposed it was possible, but I'd feel like such an idiot. What would I tell Sharon and Dad? "Never mind. These gifts were just a joke!" They'd think I was crazy. Dawn and Jeff would be here by Monday. They'd see all the gifts too.

Calm down, I urged myself. *So what if you have to pay a little interest?* How bad could it be?

It would probably be a good idea to find out.

I used the phone in Sharon and Dad's room to call Stacey. "What's the matter, Mary Anne?" she asked. "You sound panicked."

"A little, maybe," I admitted. "What do you know about interest?" As she spoke, my heart sank. She told me that most store credit cards charge interest between fourteen and twenty-two percent.

Then she calculated twenty-two percent of the sum total of my purchases. "Are you kidding?" I gasped. "I'll have to keep working and working just to pay the interest!"

"Kind of, yeah," Stacey said.

I thanked her, then hung up, stunned. There was only one answer. I had to get my hands on enough money to pay the full bill in two weeks. But how?

CHAPTER 4

That night, I took out the BSC record book and did some math of my own. I checked how much I'd earned in the last two months. I'd earned a lot more in November than I had in October, probably because people start going out more once the holiday season begins, which is before Thanksgiving.

I'd probably earn the same amount in the next two weeks as I'd earned during the first two weeks of December.

It wasn't nearly enough.

I needed another source of income. I didn't want to borrow it, and, besides, there wasn't anyone I could think of to borrow from. I lay in my bed, staring at the ceiling, worrying until almost one in the morning. Even though I exhausted my brain, I drifted off to sleep without an answer.

In the morning, though, I had an idea. I remembered Kristy commenting on the fact that

31

the mall was still looking for Christmas help so late in the season.

I'd get a job at the mall!

"What are you up to this morning?" Dad asked at breakfast as he ate his granola, a health food Sharon had converted him to.

"The mall," I replied, popping in a toaster waffle.

"Mary Anne!" Dad said sternly. "How many more —"

My laugh stopped him. "I'm done, Dad. Really."

He gazed at me, seeming to want more explanation. Should I tell him the truth? What if he wouldn't let me work at the mall? Dad's always been pretty strict. He's loosened up a lot since marrying Sharon, but that side of him is still there.

Something told me he might not approve of my working at the mall. However, I knew he was serious about paying off the interest. He would consider it *irresponsible parenting* to let me off the hook. Plus, he's a lawyer. He's big on people fulfilling their agreements to the letter of the law.

The job would only be for a few weeks. It wasn't as if I wanted to commit a crime or skip school or do anything wrong. I only wanted to work. Where was the harm in that?

"I'm just meeting some of my friends there,"

I answered him, buttering my waffle as if it were the most fascinating thing I'd ever done.

"Are you sure you're not going to buy more gifts?"

"Dad, you have the credit card," I reminded him. "I gave it back to you."

"Yes, but I don't want you spending the money you've earmarked for paying off what you charged," he said. "That's how people get in trouble with credit cards all the time. They can't pay and then the interest mounts."

Interest again! If I heard the word one more time I'd scream.

"No, I'm just going along as company this time," I assured him.

Sharon stuck her head in the kitchen doorway. "I'm off to the Nutrition Center," she reported brightly. "I want to make sure I have all the things Dawn and Jeff like. Do either of you want me to pick up anything?"

Dad and I shot one another a laughing glance, like there was even a *chance.* "No, dear," Dad said, suppressing a smile. "I don't think there's anything Mary Anne and I require from the Nutrition Center today."

Sharon knew he was teasing her and she smiled at him.

"I'd like a ride," I said. "The mall isn't too far from the center."

"Sure, come on," Sharon said.

It was nice having Sharon to myself during the ride. In a few days, Dawn and Jeff would occupy her entire universe. She missed them so much. It had taken awhile to think of Sharon as my mom, but it was starting to happen. My own mother died when I was very little. I barely remember her. It feels good having a mother, and Sharon is a great stepmom.

She dropped me off at the front of the mall and then went on to do her shopping. I hurried directly to the sign by the Christmas tree. It said to apply at the special-events office, but I didn't know where that was.

The platform by the tree was nearly completed. A man was painting gold trim on a railing that led to Santa's throne. I asked him where the office was and he directed me to a doorway behind the food court.

Once I arrived at the food court, it was easy to find the office. Lots of people were going in and out. I followed their trail to a small office. The woman at the desk handed me an application. "Return it and then stick around for an interview," she instructed me, without even looking up from her desk.

I smiled at her, but she didn't notice. So I sat on a brown couch by a door to fill out the application. I'd written down my name, address, social security number, and age when a girl sat down beside me, an application in her hand.

"Man, what a crab," she said, nodding toward the woman at the desk.

I looked up at her. She was petite, about sixteen, with short, frizzy red hair framing her face like a kind of halo. Her flawless skin and fine features were so delicate she would have reminded me of an angel, except that her bright green eyes were heavily rimmed with smudgy eye makeup.

"She's busy, I guess," I commented.

"Too busy to even look at you?"

I shrugged. Some people are like that. I figured there wasn't much sense being bothered by it. I went back to my application, but in seconds the girl rapped on my paper with a long blue-polished fingernail. "Hey, just so you know — you can't do that."

"Do what?" I asked, puzzled.

"I was looking at your application," she explained. Glancing at the woman behind the desk, she moved closer to me and whispered, "You can't tell them you're thirteen."

"I can't?"

She shook her head.

"Why not?"

"They'll never hire you." She took the pen from my hand and expertly turned the three into a six so my application said I was sixteen.

"Wow," I said, impressed by her handiwork. "You did that well."

"I've been doing it since I was thirteen. Now that I'm seventeen, I'm working on turning sevens into eights. I'm pretty good at that too." She put out her hand and I shook it. "Hi, I'm Angela."

"Mary Anne."

"Well, Mary Anne, I hope we both get a job."

"Thanks," I said.

I wasn't sure how I felt about what I was doing. It's not like me to be dishonest. And today I'd already lied to Dad. Now I was lying on an application. It didn't feel right to me. It *wasn't* right. But who was I hurting? No one. Surely I could perform any job as well as a sixteen-year-old.

Still, I wasn't sure I wanted to hand in the application. It felt too dishonest. I put the paper down on the table by the couch and stood up. " 'Bye," I murmured to Angela, who was working intently on her application.

I was at the door when Angela called to me. "Hey, Mary Anne!" Turning, I saw her by the reception desk. "You forgot to hand in your application. I handed it in for you."

"You did?"

"Sure. You can't expect them to come out and look for it."

"Thanks," I said, feeling foolish.

The receptionist looked over at me for the

first time. "Ms. Spier, you can see Ms. Cerasi now."

I stood, frozen. What should I do?

"Go!" Angela urged. "Go on."

I saw a door by the couch with the name DAWN CERASI printed on it. "There?" I asked the receptionist.

"Go right in," she said, handing my application back to me.

The door was ajar. I pushed it open and stepped in. A very professional-looking woman with short, highlighted hair and a blue business suit sat behind a desk. She shot me a quick, polite smile. "Hi," I said. "I'm Mary Anne Spier. I have a sister named Dawn, a stepsister, actually, but we're very close."

"Have you got your application?" she asked.

I blushed. She couldn't have cared less that I have a sister named Dawn. Forget passing for sixteen. She probably thought I was ten.

I handed the application to her and she told me to sit. With darting eyes, she scanned the form. "When are you available?" she asked.

"Uh, weekends and after school, but not Mondays, Wednesdays, or Fridays."

She gave me a hard look.

"I have another job," I explained quickly, which was actually true. "By the way, what job am I applying for?"

"Didn't you know? We need helpers at Winter World."

That sounded great. "I have a lot of experience with kids," I volunteered. "I love them and I baby-sit all the time." Uh-oh, did that make me sound young again? I decided it might be best just to keep my mouth shut and answer her questions.

"That will certainly help," she said, seeming to note it on my form. "Allergies?"

"Excuse me?" I asked.

"Are you allergic to anything?"

"Uh . . . no. I don't think so. I mean, not that I know of." Why didn't I just say no? I was so nervous, that's why. I'd never met anyone so businesslike.

She asked me several more questions, then asked me to stand up and turn around. I thought this was sort of odd, but I did it. "Can you start tomorrow at ten?" she asked.

"Yes!" I cried. Despite my efforts to seem grown-up, I smiled eagerly. "You mean I've got the job?"

"Congratulations. You can pick your costume up tomorrow at Winter World."

Costume?

Saturday

As soon as I told Charlotte Johanssen about Kristy's bright idea for helping the Toys for Kids program, she found a way to make the plan work in her favor. After I finished laughing, I had to set her straight about the real spirit of giving.

That Saturday morning, while I was at the mall, Stacey received a phone call from a very excited Kristy. "I've got it!" she told Stacey. "I know how we can help the Toys for Kids program. I want you to tell Dr. Johanssen as soon as you get to her house to baby-sit."

"Tell her what?" Stacey asked.

"How we're going to save the program!"

Stacey smiled. Kristy could never be happy merely assisting or lending a hand. No. She had to go full out and *save the program*! Well, that was Kristy, and she was never going to change.

Kristy then laid out her plan. The BSC would hold a fair as a holiday fund-raiser. "We'll call it Santa-Hanukkah-Kwanzaa Town," she explained.

"We don't have a fortune in the treasury," Stacey pointed out.

"I thought of that," Kristy replied. There were two parts to her plan. First, we would collect donations of canned food and second-hand toys for the fair. "We can use the old toys for prizes and use the food donations to make refreshments," she explained. Then, after the fair, we'd use the money we earned to buy new toys for the kids.

"Dr. Johanssen can arrive at her meeting today knowing that we're going to be doing this," Kristy went on. "Then she'll know what else, if anything, she needs to do."

"It sounds good," Stacey said. "I bet she'll be happy to hear the news."

The moment Stacey arrived at Charlotte's she told Dr. Johanssen the news. Dr. Johanssen was more than happy. She was thrilled!

"Leave it to you girls!" she said warmly. "No one gets things done like the BSC members do."

"It's not done yet," Stacey said with a slightly nervous smile. It would be a big job, and everyone was already busy with holiday activities. But she also knew that once Kristy set her mind to something, it usually happened.

"Stacey!" Charlotte cried, bouncing down the stairs. She's eight and adores Stacey. The two of them have become very close. "I got a fashion-maker program for my computer," she told Stacey. "You can make real fashions and then print out the pattern on actual cloth with color and everything."

"Awesome," Stacey said. "You have to show me."

"Before I leave, tell me Kristy's plan," Dr. Johanssen said as she took her coat from the front closet. Charlotte listened with increasing interest as Stacey told her what she knew.

"This sounds fun!" Charlotte cried. "Maybe we can have a fashion booth."

"Good idea," Stacey agreed.

"Charlotte, I'm sure you can gather some old toys to donate," said her mother. Stacey knew that was true. Charlotte is an only child and she has a mountain of toys. Charlotte wasn't as convinced, though.

She squinted thoughtfully, as if envisioning her toy collection. "I'll look," she said, diplomatically evading the issue.

"Excellent," said Dr. Johanssen as she wrote down the phone number for the hospital conference room where she was holding the meeting of volunteers. Stacey already knew the number of her cellular phone. "This will give us entirely new information to work with," she added. "You're *definitely* going to do this, aren't you?"

"Definitely," Stacey assured her with a smile.

"Mom, can I pick out some food for us to donate?" Charlotte asked as Dr. Johanssen opened the door.

"Of course," her mother replied. "We have to do our part too."

As soon as she left, Charlotte grabbed Stacey's wrist and pulled her toward the kitchen. "We have a ton of food for you," she said.

"Don't you want to show me your fashion program first?" Stacey asked.

"No," Charlotte replied firmly. "This is more important. We can do that later."

42

She found a box by the cellar stairs and pulled open a nearby cabinet. "Olives, definitely," she said, placing the can of olives in the carton. Next she found two tins of anchovies. "Yechh!" she said, putting them in the box. "Let's get these out of the house for sure."

"You don't like anchovies?" Stacey asked, fighting back a smile.

Charlotte twisted her face into such a look of revulsion that Stacey burst into laughter. "I guess not," she said with a chuckle.

Charlotte pulled can after can from the various shelves. "Beets have to go for sure. Ew, we even have pickled beets. You can have those, too. Corn relish — disgusting. You can have that. And this tin of paté stuff will kill you. That's yours."

In no time, Charlotte had loaded the box with all the food products she loathed. The list included: canned white asparagus, a jar of oyster sauce, cardboard drums of wheat germ, oatmeal, and puffed rice.

"Can you take frozen stuff?" she asked, pulling open the freezer. "We have loads of spinach and brussels sprouts." She took a box of brussels sprouts from the freezer. "Have you ever tasted these?" she asked.

Stacey nodded. "Yes."

Charlotte winced and made the revolted face

again. "Oh, man," she moaned. "Eating brussels sprouts is like eating dirt."

"I kind of like them," Stacey said, laughing.

"You do not!" Charlotte refused to believe such a thing could be possible.

"Your parents like them," Stacey pointed out.

"They're grown-ups!" Charlotte gestured toward her box of hated foods. "They like all this stuff. They're crazy."

Stacey stooped down to the box, sorting through it. She smiled and had to admit that she didn't like most of the things in there either. "Charlotte, Kristy and I didn't discuss it, but I don't think this is the sort of stuff she's looking for."

Charlotte's face fell in disappointment. "It was too good to be true," she said glumly. "What does she want?"

"I guess we'll want things like tomato sauce for making chili, or ingredients for cakes and cookies, snacks, sodas — stuff like that."

"Foods people will actually *want* to eat, you mean?" Charlotte said, nodding. "I understand."

With a deep sigh of resignation, Charlotte returned the cans to their shelves.

When the box was empty, Charlotte sat cross-legged on the kitchen floor, opened a cabinet, and stared into it wistfully. "I suppose you'd like this brownie mix," she said after a moment, pulling the box from a bottom shelf.

"That would be good," Stacey agreed, kneeling beside Charlotte.

"Might as well take this icing," Charlotte said reluctantly. "This bag of potato chips will probably help too," she added, sighing again as she plunked it into the carton. "Here's a box of Yodels. I suppose someone will love them as much as I do."

Stacey rubbed Charlotte's arm comfortingly. "You know, Char," she said, "what you're doing now is in the real spirit of holiday giving. You're thinking about what would really be helpful instead of only giving away things you don't want."

Charlotte's eyes brightened at Stacey's words. "Mom and Dad would just buy more anchovies and pickled beets anyway," she said philosophically.

"They'll buy more brownie mix, too," Stacey said.

"You're right," said Charlotte brightly. "So it really doesn't matter what we give. We'll just get more! Take everything!"

"I don't need everything," Stacey told her with a smile. "If everyone donates a little, then we'll have plenty."

Once again, Charlotte was filled with enthusiasm. "You're right. Let's go all around the neighborhood and ask everyone to give us something. We'll have a ton of stuff in no time."

"Good idea," Stacey said, getting up too. "Do you think a lot of people are home now?"

"Wait! Wait! I have a better idea!" Charlotte cried. "We'll write something on my computer to let people know what we're doing. We'll tell them to bring their food and toys here."

"Great idea! We can print up flyers and leave them for people who aren't home."

Charlotte called Dr. Johanssen and received permission to use the house as a drop-off point for donations. Stacey told me later that she felt very proud of Charlotte and herself. She felt as though they were thinking like Kristy, coming up with brilliant ideas on their own.

She and Charlotte bundled up and got Charlotte's wagon from the garage. They headed out to ask for donations. At almost every house, they were warmly met and loaded with both food and toys. They left their flyers at homes where no one answered the door. Several times, they had to return to the Johanssens' to unload before starting out again. "What a great beginning," Stacey said to Charlotte. "Our fund-raiser is off to a fabulous start!"

CHAPTER 6

Getting to the mall Sunday morning to report for my first day of work was a challenge. Dad and Sharon were full of questions and concerns.

"Mary Anne, you *know* how I feel about those kids who spend all their free time at the mall," Dad said to me at breakfast. He sat up straight, frowned, and looked as authoritative as possible. "What do they call them? Mall cats?"

"Mall rats," Sharon corrected him.

I stifled a smile.

"Whatever," Dad went on sternly. "You are not to be hanging out at the mall."

"I'm not," I said as I tucked my white blouse into my newest jeans for the zillionth time. I kept tucking it in and taking it out, unable to decide which looked better. I wanted to look just right on my first day of work.

"I hope you're not buying more gifts," Sharon put in more mildly.

"I'm not spending more money and I'm not hanging out," I assured them.

"Then, exactly what are you doing?" Dad asked.

The moment I'd been dreading had come. "Um . . . my friends and I are helping Dr. Johanssen with the Toys for Kids program. We're getting donations."

It consoled me a little that this was at least a small bit true. The lie was that I let Dad and Sharon assume this was taking place at the mall, which, of course, it wasn't.

Dad relaxed. "How wonderful," Sharon said. "I'll drive you there."

"It's all right. I'll take the bus." Taking a ride from Sharon would have made me feel terrible. Besides, she might have decided to come into the mall with me and that would have been a disaster.

"Are you sure?" she asked.

"Really. We're all taking the bus together."

"All right. I can't fit everyone into the car."

"Yeah . . . well . . . I've got to go."

It was a cold day and the bus took forever to arrive, since it was on a Sunday schedule. In my seat, gazing out the window, I wondered about the costume I would be wearing.

It had to be a uniform of some kind, not a costume. I remembered that last year the people who took the pictures of the kids with

Santa wore identical blue slacks and white shirts. That was probably what Ms. Cerasi had meant.

When the bus finally arrived, it was five to ten. I dashed through the mall entrance, running toward the Winter World platform. The mall was still coming to life. Most of the stores were gated, though you could see salespeople inside.

Winter World was now complete and it looked great. Brightly painted castle towers stood around the platform. Santa's throne was positioned in the front doorway of the castle. Automated reindeer were placed here and there, their heads moving. Holidays songs played from speakers hidden somewhere in the castle. Winter World was enclosed by a gold fence.

Santa wasn't on his throne yet, but a big sign announced his arrival. SANTA ARRIVES TODAY! it declared. HOLIDAY PARADE AT ELEVEN! FREE GIFTS! BALLOONS! HALF-PRICE PHOTOS!

Eleven! I thought, panicked. I had to get moving. Frantically, I checked around for someone to supply me with my uniform.

"Young lady," someone called. A woman was coming toward me from a nearby store. It was the unfriendly receptionist from the day before. "You're a helper, aren't you?" she asked. I nodded and she handed me a large white shopping bag that was stapled shut on top. "Hurry and put this on," she instructed me. "You're going to assist in the Welcome Santa parade. Report to the front mall entrance once you're dressed."

The bag was huge and a little heavy. What kind of outfit was this? "Where do I change?" I asked.

"The female employees' lounge beside the ladies' room on the third floor."

Even though I was curious about the costume, I was too anxious about being on time to stop and check it out. I took the elevator to the third floor, found the rest room, and spotted a door marked EMPLOYEES ONLY. I felt very cool going in there, as if I were someone important.

The pink walls of the room were lined with lockers. Two tables sat in the middle. A soda machine and snack machine stood in a corner. A ladies' room was on the right.

"Hi!" a voice cried. I turned and saw Angela, wearing only a bra and slip.

"Hi," I replied with a smile. "You got the job too. Great!"

"Yeah, I really need it. Let's see your costume."

I ripped open the bag and was so startled by the sight inside that I jumped back. "What is that?" I exclaimed.

Angela started laughing so hard she had to

lean against one of the tables for support. "Your face!" she gasped. "I wish I had a camera!"

I crept back to the bag and peered inside. Two huge eyes stared back at me. It was a head. I lifted it from the bag. Under the big eyes was a button nose and a wide smile. "What's it supposed to be?" I asked.

"An elf," Angela told me cheerfully. She reached into the bag and pulled out pointed green slippers, a green tunic, and a pair of green tights.

"An elf," I echoed in disbelief.

"Didn't you know what job you were applying for?" Angela asked.

"Well, I knew it was for a *helper*."

"Yeah, *Santa's* helper. Didn't you notice that everyone applying for the job was on the short side? Look at me. Without heels, I'm a shrimp."

Standing there in her bare feet, Angela did look shorter than she had the day before. I guess I'd been too nervous then to pay attention to the other people around me.

"Don't look so upset about it," Angela said with a laugh. "This is the best job in the world. You get to hang out with cute little kids. Imagine if you were a salesclerk or a stock girl. Then you'd *really* be working! This is fun."

She was right, of course. But all I could think about was the embarrassment. What if someone saw me? Thank goodness for the elf head. At least I'd be able to hide inside it. If anyone found out I was doing this, I'd die of humiliation.

No one could ever know about this — not Kristy, not Dawn, not Logan. Especially not Logan! Sure, he'd be nice about it and not tease me *too* much, but every time he'd look at me he'd see this goofy, grinning elf person. Not exactly romantic.

"You'd better put that thing on," Angela said as she pulled on her own tights. "You don't want to be late for the parade."

There was nothing to do but put on the costume. I stuck the elf head under my arm and started for the door. "Wait!" Angela cried. "You have to put that on in here. Ms. Cerasi told me no one can be seen in half costume. It's a big no-no."

"Okay," I agreed. I didn't want anyone to see me anyway. I lowered the mask over my head, and adjusted it so I could see out the screen located in the elf's big smile. Then I headed for the door and banged into a locker. "Ow!" I cried.

Angela hurried to me, wobbling slightly under the weight of her mask, which was like mine but with a slightly different face. Clasping my shoulders, she steered me toward the door: "It takes some getting used to," she said, her voice muffled by her mask.

No kidding! My side vision was almost completely cut off and I couldn't see anything directly under me.

We stumbled through the mall, banging into guard rails, people, each other, and anything else we couldn't quite see. Not only was my field of vision narrow, but the head itself threw me off balance, tipping first to one side, then to the other as it slid along my shoulders. And my pointy elf slippers were a bit big, with smooth soles that slid on the polished floor.

The mall was beginning to fill up. Kids we passed shouted to us excitedly as we waved, which was fun. "Hey, look — it's Dopey! Two of them!" a kid shouted to his mother.

We waved again as we stepped into the elevator.

"Dopey is exactly how I feel," I muttered, pressing the down button.

"Aw, lighten up." Angela laughed. "This is a blast."

By the time we reached the front entrance we were walking much more steadily. We entered a large tent that had been set up in front of the doors. Inside, we met three more elves. I assumed they were guys since I hadn't seen them in the dressing room. Ms. Cerasi was there.

"Elves, you'll carry Santa's sled," she instructed us in the same no-nonsense tone she'd used during my interview. The five of us lifted a plywood sled with an open bottom. It wasn't very heavy.

"Wait," said a man in a Santa suit. "I have to get into the sled." We lowered the sled so he could step inside.

He was a great-looking Santa. He had a genuine long white beard, not a fake one. He didn't seem to be padded with pillows either. He was an authentic old, fat guy with twinkly, happy eyes.

"Where are my reindeer?" Ms. Cerasi asked.

Three tall, slim people in full reindeer costumes, complete with huge antlers, pranced into position in front of the sled. Various other fairies, dancing candy canes, nutcrackers, and ornaments took their places.

Angela leaned toward me, holding her mask in place. Her voice sounded faraway from behind the screen. "We're lucky. A lot of these people were only hired to work this one day."

"Yeah, lucky," I agreed, even though I wasn't so sure. When you're trying to hold a job secretly, you don't want one that requires you to stand in the middle of the biggest mall in the area.

A recorded blare of horns sounded. "All

right, everyone, march!" Ms. Cerasi commanded, holding open the tent's flap.

I took a deep breath and started walking. The moment we emerged from the tent, the crowd of people who'd assembled began to cheer.

And that was how I began my secret life as an elf.

CHAPTER 7

Thank goodness my parents had given me permission to stay home from school on Monday. Dawn and Jeff's flight was due in and they knew I'd want to meet the plane.

As it turned out, though, I was completely exhausted from my first day as an elf. You wouldn't believe how my neck and shoulders hurt. My legs, too. All day I'd had to squat to eye level with kids who were nervous about seeing Santa.

Really little kids (three years old and under, mostly) aren't always sure they want to get so close to the strange man dressed in red. Some of them have never even seen a man with a beard before, so that alone is weird for them. They cling to their parents. But the parents — some of them — are determined to get a picture of their child on Santa's lap, so they keep urging the kid to go see him.

Instinctively, when I see a crying child, I

want to help. So I kept stooping down to comfort them and make them stop crying.

I personally didn't care if they went to see Santa or not. But Ms. Cerasi did. And I got lucky. Just as Ms. Cerasi was cruising by, coolly checking on how things were going, I set a kid down and he said (loudly) to his mother, "The elf is my friend, Mommy. I see Santa now."

Way to go, kid!

For the first time, Ms. Cerasi beamed a smile my way. "Well handled," she said. "I see you *do* know children."

From behind my mask, there wasn't much I could do in response but wave and nod to her. But privately I was grinning.

"What's wrong with your neck?" Sharon asked.

Her question startled me. I wasn't rubbing it or anything. "Nothing. Why?"

"You keep rolling your head," she explained.

I hadn't realized I was doing that. "I must be a little stiff from sleeping."

"Oh . . . well . . . hurry and eat. We have to get to the airport," she said.

The ride to the airport takes about two hours in morning rush-hour traffic. It went fast because I snoozed in the backseat. When I awoke, Dad was parking in the airport lot.

Inside the terminal, we checked the flight schedule, then hurried to the gate where Jeff and Dawn's plane was arriving. "Dawn! Dawn!" I shouted as soon as I spied her in the crowd of deplaning passengers.

She turned and shot me that great smile of hers. Her teeth seemed especially dazzling. And, as she approached, her eyes appeared somehow bluer. It was probably because she was tanner than the last time I had seen her. Her hair looked blonder too.

Dawn and Jeff first hugged Sharon, who squeezed them tight. Then Dawn turned to me. "Mary Anne, hi."

It was an odd moment. I lunged forward to wrap her in a hug — and she jumped. "Oh, sorry," she said, and laughed uncomfortably. "I wasn't expecting that." She recovered instantly, then hugged me. But it felt awkward. Forced, in a way. It left me with an uneasy feeling.

Next, I hugged Jeff, who seemed the same as ever — easygoing, slightly gawky, friendly. He was a smidge taller than at Thanksgiving, but otherwise he seemed unchanged.

"Anybody hungry?" Dad asked.

"I can wait until we get home," Dawn replied. "Can we go to Cabbages and Kings?" she asked, naming her favorite health food restaurant in Stoneybrook.

"Absolutely," said Dad. "We'll get your luggage and head back right away."

On the ride home, Dawn seemed quiet. She

talked a little about Vista, her school. At Vista the eighth-graders are in the same building as the high schoolers, and I could tell she was impressed by the older students.

"I'm not sure I like that arrangement," Sharon said.

"Oh, it's really cool, Mom," Dawn insisted. "By the time you're in eighth grade, you're really too old to be hanging around with sixth- and seventh-graders anyway."

"Mary Anne doesn't mind it," Sharon argued.

Dawn looked to me for confirmation. I thought of Jessi and Mallory, who are in sixth grade. And Claudia has been in seventh grade until recently. "It doesn't bother me," I admitted.

The expression on Dawn's face was difficult to read. It wasn't an actual frown. It was more as if she were studying my face and coming to some unflattering conclusion about it. "Oh, well," she said after a moment. "Everyone's different. But I love being with the older kids. It's so much more interesting to me."

Jeff jumped in with stories about the surfing lessons he's taking at the beach near where they live. His stories made Sharon so worried that she forgot her worries about Dawn in high school.

During our lunch at Cabbages and Kings, I felt as though I couldn't connect with Dawn.

For one thing, she wasn't making eye contact with me. It's almost impossible to feel close to someone when he or she won't look you in the eye. Dawn was just holding everyone in a kind of group gaze, which unnerved me. I desperately wanted that connection back.

This was Dawn, my best friend, my stepsister. The person I'd been looking forward to seeing. Maybe she was just tired, I told myself. After all, I hadn't just taken a six-hour flight. She had. Or perhaps something was on her mind that she'd confide in me when we were alone.

I clung to that thought for the rest of the afternoon as Dawn continued to seem friendly but distant.

We went to the BSC meeting together and everyone showered her with affection and questions. Again, I had that left-out feeling, but I blamed myself for being childish. I wasn't Dawn's only friend. Everyone else was excited to see her, as well. I couldn't expect her to pay special attention to me.

That night, though, I figured my time had come. I finally had her all to myself. As we got ready for bed, I wandered into her room. "So," I said, stretching out on her bed. "How's everything?"

She was unpacking, putting clothing into her dresser. "I told you, great," she answered.

But I wanted the real story, not the public, parent-approved version. I wanted to hear about boyfriends, girlfriends, parents, everything. Sure, Dawn and I spoke on the phone all the time. But the phone isn't as personal as talking alone and face-to-face. This was a moment I'd looked forward to for a long time, and it was going nowhere. "Anything exciting happening?" I tried again.

"Lots of things, but nothing really amazing," she replied. "How about you?"

Oh, nothing, I'm an elf, I thought.

At that moment, I might have told her about my job, but since she wasn't sharing anything, I didn't feel like sharing either. Instead, I told her about the Santa-Hanukkah-Kwanzaa Town fund-raiser. No one had mentioned it during the meeting, since we'd all been busy talking to her, and the phone had rung constantly with clients requesting sitters.

I thought she'd have a million questions about our project. Instead, she just smiled an amused little smile. "You guys are always helping someone," she commented lightly.

"Don't you and your friends do things for anyone else?" I asked defensively. I didn't like her tone of voice. What was wrong with helping people?

"Things are different where I am," she said. "We're more laid-back. Not so gung ho."

"Oh, excuse me," I said sourly.

She realized she'd offended me and smiled apologetically. "Come on, Mary Anne. You know how my school is. It's not like we don't care. We just did a Save the Whales project. The seniors actually took boats out in the ocean so people could observe the humpbacks, and they donated the money they made to the Whale Foundation. It's just that we do things in a more casual way."

The way she kept using the word *we* really bugged me. *We* were we — she and I. Or Dawn and the BSC. She and a bunch of "laid-back" high school kids weren't *we*.

At that exact moment, I suddenly couldn't stand being in the room with her. The urge to shake her until she became the old Dawn again was almost overwhelming. "Good night," I said, sliding off the bed.

"Mary Anne . . ." Her voice stopped me as I reached the door.

I turned toward her. "What?"

"I think what you guys are doing for the kids is great. Honestly. I'm just tired, I suppose."

My angry feelings melted. "Sure. You had a long day." Dawn would rest and the next day would be better. The old closeness would return and everything would be okay.

Only it didn't return and everything wasn't

okay. In the morning, she seemed just as far away.

My zooming new schedule didn't help matters. I was scheduled to work on Tuesday after school.

That morning I'd told everyone I was going to the mall to work on the BSC fund-raiser. "I'll drive you there, Dawn," Sharon said. "Then you can join your friends."

"I don't really feel like it," Dawn replied. (Inwardly I sighed with relief.)

"You probably still have jet lag," said Sharon.

"That's probably it," Dawn agreed.

Annoyed as I was by Dawn's lack of desire to spend time with my friends and me, it was a lucky break. What would I have done if she'd wanted to meet us? I suppose I could have told her my secret, but I wasn't in the mood.

I arrived at the mall in time to change with the earlier shift of elves. The "ancient gnomes," Angela called them, giggling mischievously. It might not have been a nice thing to call them, but it was hard not to laugh. Most of the day elves were retired people. They were great with the kids, but they didn't do a lot of sprightly dancing around the way Ms. Cerasi wanted us to.

During my shift, I had several close calls.

Mrs. Rodowsky, one of our regular clients, showed up with her four-year-old son, Archie. All the while he was in line, Archie kept staring at me. Had he recognized me? It was possible. I'd sat for his brothers and him just the week before. Could he see me through the screen? I kept turning my big plastic head away from him.

After he'd finished visiting Santa (whose real name was Marv Howard), Archie made a beeline for me. I froze, not knowing what to do or say.

"Mom, doesn't this elf look like my Dopey doll?" he said excitedly.

Whew!

I waved and danced around in as sprightly a way as I could manage, considering I felt I was going to faint with relief. Archie hugged me and I patted his head.

I saw several other clients and their kids. None seemed to recognize me, though. By the end of my shift I was tired. The mask was hot and heavy. Plus, all that sprightly dancing, stooping, bending, and waving was exhausting.

When I noticed Angela leave the platform, I knew our shift was up. I wondered why she didn't wait for me, but figured she was as hot and tired as I was.

"Thank goodness," I cried, bursting into the

employees' lounge and pulling off my mask. Shaking out my sweaty hair, I looked around for Angela but didn't spot her. "Angela?" I called softly.

There was no reply. She couldn't have changed that quickly. "Angela, are you here?"

Strange, I thought. She could have stopped off at a number of places, though, so I didn't worry. Eager to splash cold water on my face, I headed for the bathroom. Before I even opened the door, I heard sobs coming from inside.

I pushed open the door. Angela stood in front of the sink, mopping her red, tear-stained face with one of the rough bathroom towels. Her heavy eye makeup was all over her cheeks. "Angela?" I cried, alarmed. "What happened?"

"Nothing," she said quickly. "It's really nothing."

"Then why are you crying?" I asked.

"It's so stupid I don't even want to talk about it," she insisted, turning toward the mirror and attempting to wipe the makeup from her cheeks with her knuckles.

"Are you sure?"

"Absolutely. Don't even worry. It's nothing."

I wished I could believe her. But I didn't.

CHAPTER 8

The rest of the week can only be described by one word — insane. I should have slept in my sneakers because all I did was run. After school I ran to the mall, or to a BSC meeting, or to a sitting job. Then I'd zoom home and rush through my homework before I crash-landed into my bed.

Then, one day, a miracle occurred. I got a day off.

One of the "ancient gnomes" (who were actually very nice people) was looking for extra elfing hours, so Ms. Cerasi asked me if I'd mind giving up one of my shifts. "No problem," I told her. I desperately needed a break.

"Hi, Mary Anne. 'Bye, Mary Anne," Dawn said to me in the hall on Friday evening as I passed her on the way to my bedroom.

"Hi, how's everything going?" I asked, leaning against the wall for support. That's how tired I was.

"Fine, but what's happening with you? I never see you."

At least she'd noticed. "I'm off tomorrow," I told her.

"What do you mean 'off'?"

Oops. "I mean . . . uh . . . no homework, no BSC . . . no baby-sitting. Amazing, huh?"

"Yeah," she agreed. "Good. We can do something together."

Oops again. "I promised Logan I'd spend some time with him. Do you mind if he hangs out with us?"

Dawn frowned. "I don't mind, but will *he* mind?"

I wasn't sure. "He'll have to understand," I said, too weary to worry about it.

"Okay, then. If you're sure. What should we do?"

"We should think about it tomorrow," I replied. My brain wasn't doing any more thinking just then.

That day I'd gone to school, filled in for Angela at the mall for an hour and a half because she was going to be late, hurried back for a BSC meeting, and then run along with Mallory to a sitting job for the Barrett-DeWitt kids afterward.

After talking to Dawn, I hit the bed and was instantly involved in the weirdest dream. The Seven Dwarfs came to my house and demanded all my Christmas purchases back because I couldn't pay for them. They marched into the house and took them from under the tree. I chased them out into the front yard, where I met Angela dressed as Snow White. She was crying because the Wicked Queen was after her. I looked up in the sky and saw Ms. Cerasi dressed as a witch, flying overhead on a broom. Grabbing Angela's hand, I rushed back to the house, but the door was locked. I peered through the front window and could see Dawn inside, and though I frantically rapped on the glass, she wouldn't let me in.

In the middle of the night, I woke up, relieved to discover it was all a dream. But when I fell asleep again, I dreamed the Barrett-DeWitt kids were chasing me down Burnt Hill Road (my street), throwing tree ornaments at me. They were laughing, as though it were all in fun, but I couldn't make them stop.

I woke up the next day exhausted from all that dreaming. When I glanced at my clock, I was in for a shock. It was almost noon! I'd promised Logan I'd phone him by ten. I pulled on my robe, dashed out of my room, and ran down the stairs.

At the bottom of the stairs, I heard Logan's voice. For a moment I thought I was still dreaming. Then I realized his voice was coming from the kitchen. He was talking to Dawn.

"No, don't wake her," he said. "I'll come back later."

"I'm up! I'm awake!" I cried, hurrying into the kitchen.

"Hey, sleepyhead," Dawn greeted me. "I was just about to come up and get you out of bed. Logan is nicer. He said you were exhausted and we should let you sleep."

Logan smiled. "When you didn't call, I figured I'd just come over and get you. Since you were sleeping, though, I thought you ought to rest. You've been so busy lately I know you must be tired."

"Thanks for letting me sleep," I said, patting down my mussed-up morning-hair. "I needed it. But I'm okay now. What do you guys want to do today?"

"We've already decided," Dawn said. "Logan and I are both way behind on our Christmas shopping. We *have* to go to Washington Mall."

"No!" I gasped. "Not there!"

"What's wrong with the mall all of a sudden?" Dawn asked pointedly. "You spend every minute at the mall. I thought you were the mall's biggest fan."

"That's . . . uh . . . the problem," I stammered. "I'm sick of it. I've been there too much."

"I know. You have a secret boyfriend at the

mall," Logan teased. "You don't want me to meet him."

"Don't be silly," I snapped, even though I knew he was kidding. He'd come unnervingly close to the truth. I didn't have a secret boyfriend. But I did have a secret life.

"If you don't have a secret boyfriend, then why can't we go?" said Dawn. "Mary Anne, I really need to shop. Come on."

"I'll take you to see Santa," Logan teased.

I froze. "I'll go only if you promise *not* to take me to see Santa," I replied.

"It's a deal," Logan said, rising from his chair. "Let's go."

All through the bus ride I felt jittery. I kept up a steady patter of the stupidest conversation you could imagine. I even resorted to knock-knock jokes. "Knock-knock."

"Who's there?" Logan played along, rolling his eyes. This was my sixth knock-knock.

"Venice."

"Venice who?"

"Ven is these stupid knock-knocks ever going to end?"

"That's exactly what I've been wondering," Dawn said dryly. I smiled, but she didn't seem to be joking. Okay, maybe knock-knocks aren't exactly fascinating, but they're not torture either.

"Sorry," I said. "Are knock-knocks too immature for you, now that you're in high school?" What can I tell you? She was getting on my nerves.

"Oh, yeah. I remember. You told me about that at Thanksgiving. You're in high school," Logan said, diffusing the potential argument. (He probably did it on purpose. Logan is like that.) "How's that going?"

Dawn then gushed on about how awesome her school year had been so far. "It's so great not being in with the little kids anymore," she told him. Was she really turning into such a maturity snob? If I'd had my elf head, I would have hit her with it. (I'd have *liked* to, anyway. Though, I suppose that would have definitely been *immature*.)

When the bus turned into the parking lot, I saw that the mall was packed with shoppers. Total holiday madness. The moment we stepped inside, I became anxious. I don't like crowds and somehow I knew I was going to be recognized by someone. "Look at all these people. This is crazy. Let's go home," I said.

"We'll only stay a short while," Logan said, entwining his fingers through mine. "Come on."

So, I tagged along, nervously checking every store for someone who knew me, while Logan and Dawn shopped.

Logan is a careful shopper. He inspected

every item and then put it down to think about it some more before making his purchase.

Dawn is more impulsive. She was grabbing up gifts for her friends back in California. "Thank goodness I saved up for this," she said. "Otherwise I wouldn't have a dime to spend." As she took out her cash to pay for her gifts, I wished I'd done the same — saved my money and spent only what I'd saved. If I had, I wouldn't be living this weird double life now.

Dawn bought a book on modern art for her friend Amalia. She found a framed black-and-white photo of ducks on a lake at sunset for her pal Ducky. She bought a Mexican-style sun plaque for her friend Sunny, and a daisy chain belt for her friend Maggie.

I was impressed with her gifts. They seemed so . . . grown-up.

At about two-thirty, we took a lunch break at Friendly's. Dawn ordered a salad, while Logan and I ate burgers and fries. She finished while we were still eating. "I'm going to pop into that accessories store a few doors down," she said, leaving money on the table as she slid out of the booth. "I can't stand to sit here and watch you guys eat meat. I'll check back in ten minutes."

"Suit yourself," I told her coolly. She smiled, ignoring my tone of voice, and left. I turned to Logan. "Now we can eat our vile, loathsome animal product in peace."

Logan laughed. "It is good to be a carnivore," he replied in a caveman voice. "Meat, yum. Deep-fat-fried fries, yum."

"I don't know what's with her this visit," I complained, dipping a fry into ketchup.

"What do you mean?"

"It's like she's changed. She thinks she's too sophisticated to be friends with me or something."

"I didn't see that. She was dying to wake you up this morning."

"Really?"

"Yeah . . . and remember, Mary Anne, you've been so busy."

"I know," I admitted. "We've hardly spent any time together. And —" I stopped midsentence.

Ms. Cerasi was walking down the aisle toward me.

What if she stopped to speak to me? I'd have to tell Logan how I knew her.

Plus, what if she noticed that Logan looked sort of young? She might grow suspicious and want to see proof of my age. I'd lose my job and have to start paying interest to Dad.

I slid down in my seat. "Mary Anne? What's wrong?" Logan asked.

I pretended to dig frantically through my purse. "I can't find my wallet," I lied. "Maybe it fell on the floor." I slid under the table.

On my hands and knees under the table, I peered out from under the table. Ms. Cerasi had taken a seat behind us. Luckily, her back was toward us.

Logan looked under the table. "Is it there?" he asked.

I looked up at him so quickly I banged my head. "Ow! No. Let's check outside. Maybe I dropped it."

"Shouldn't we wait for Dawn?" Logan asked.

"We'll find her at the store," I whispered fiercely. "Let's go."

Logan continued to gaze at me under the table. "What?" I barked in a hoarse whisper.

"I'm waiting for you to get out of there," he explained, looking puzzled.

I crawled out from under the table, grabbed my purse, and hurried to the front of Friendly's without even waiting for him. While Logan paid, I raced out into the mall.

He joined me just as Dawn was returning. "That was fast," she commented.

"Where do you want to look first?" Logan asked.

"For what?" I said.

He squinted at me as if I'd gone nuts. "For your *wallet*."

"Oh." I laughed nervously. "I found it. It was in my bag all along. I just didn't see it."

Logan frowned. He knew something was up, but he couldn't figure out what. Dawn wanted a fruit shake at the food court, so we headed over there.

We had almost reached the concession stand when we passed Marv Howard coming from the employee area, wearing his Santa suit. He was probably finishing his lunch break. "Hi, Mary Anne," he called with a wave of his gloved hand.

"Hi, Marv," I called back without thinking.

I suddenly realized Dawn and Logan had stopped walking and were staring at me. "Santa knows your name?" Logan asked, his eyebrows raised in surprise.

I giggled nervously. "What can I say? I've been good this year."

"Marv?" Dawn said.

I shrugged and smiled feebly. "I just thought it would be funny to call him Marv."

Dawn folded her arms, peering at me suspiciously. "Mary Anne, I have to tell you this — you are developing a very odd sense of humor."

"Forget odd, I think you're losing your mind," Logan added, only half joking.

What could I tell them? Maybe they were right.

CHAPTER 9

Saturday

I'd just like to take a moment to say I'm glad that we included Kwanzaa in our holiday fund-raiser. I'm proud of this holiday celebrating my African heritage.

I know how you feel, Jessi. I feel the same way about Hanukkah. But yesterday I just wished all the holidays were over. The kids are going crazy!

On Saturday afternoon, Abby sat for Archie, Shea, and Jackie Rodowsky.

That same afternoon, Jessi had to watch Becca and Squirt because her aunt Cecelia wanted to do some shopping with Mr. and Mrs. Ramsey. (In fact, Logan, Dawn, and I ran into the three of them that day at the mall.)

Since they'd be sitting at the same time, Abby and Jessi decided to get together with their respective charges and work on Santa-Hanukkah-Kwanzaa Town.

In the week since Kristy had conceived the idea, a lot had been accomplished. We had stored tons of canned goods in Dr. Johanssen's garage. We had also collected bags and bags of old toys.

Abby took as many of those as she could carry from Kristy's garage, where they were stored, and dragged them to the Rodowskys' house with her. (It wasn't too hard because her mother drove her and helped load and unload.)

The plan was to sort through the toys and separate the good ones — which would be suitable to give away as prizes — from the more worn ones. Then they'd look through the worn-out pile and see which toys could be fixed up enough to use in such things as grab bags, fishing games, and knock-over-the-toy games. (We wouldn't donate any of *these* toys. The hospital committee was planning to use the money we earned to buy new toys for the sick kids.) We also planned to ask everyone who came to Santa-Hanukkah-Kwanzaa Town to donate a brand-new unopened toy.

Abby had proposed this at yesterday's meeting and everyone thought it was a great idea. Nothing, or very little, would be wasted. And it would involve the kids in the project.

At the same time, Kristy, Stacey, and Claudia would be at the Johanssens' house figuring out how to best use the canned goods. Kristy was also working on getting permission to use the Stoneybrook Elementary School gym for the event. All systems were ready to go.

The moment Abby opened the first bag of toys, Archie went wild. He began bouncing up and down, his carrot-top hair flying around his freckled face. "Toys! Toys! Toys!" he shouted gleefully.

"Hold on," Abby said, laughing. "These aren't for you. They're for the fund-raiser."

"A fun-raiser?" said Jackie, who is seven and who has the same carrot-colored hair his brothers have. "That sounds really good."

"No, fun*d*-raiser," Abby explained.

"Duh, Jackie," said Shea, the oldest. "*Fund*, not fun."

"We're raising money to buy toys for kids

stuck in the hospital over the holidays," Abby continued.

"Oh," Archie said, deeply disappointed. "Well, I'll only take a few, then."

"Archie, you can't have any," Abby told him gently. She explained the plan to him. As she did, the doorbell rang. Jessi had arrived with Becca and Squirt.

The moment he was in the door, Squirt made a beeline for the toys. "Mine! Mine! Mine!" he crowed happily.

Jessi and Abby exchanged anxious glances. Maybe this wasn't as good an idea as it had seemed.

Squirt is normally a very good little guy, but being torn from a bag of toys was more than he could handle. He began wailing as Jessi pried a small rubber Barney from his fingers. "That's not yours," she tried to explain, but he simply didn't understand.

"Would he play with this?" Abby offered, pulling a very used Sesame Street puzzle from the bag.

"If I help him," Jessi said.

While Jessi tried to interest Squirt in the puzzle, Becca joined Archie and Shea in sorting through the pile of toys. "Good, no good, no good, good," they said, separating them into two piles.

By the end of an hour, they had two almost

equal-sized piles. "Should we throw the no-good stuff away?" Becca asked.

"No, take it into the kitchen. We're going to be Santa's helpers and fix it up," Abby replied.

As the kids carried the beat-up toys to the kitchen, Abby followed with paints, glue, sandpaper, and other equipment she'd brought from home. "Hey, I know what to do. We can sand and paint these chipped wooden blocks," she said, surveying the hill of toys on the kitchen table. "Then we can build towers for kids to try to knock down," she added.

"Good idea!" Shea agreed. But he was the only one who had any patience for sanding. Becca, Jackie, and Archie wanted to dive into the painting. Even when Abby and Shea sanded madly, they couldn't do it fast enough.

"Don't paint yet," Abby kept telling them.

"I'm just doing a corner," Becca would insist.

Archie and Jackie began dabbing one another with the paintbrushes. "Cool it, dudes," Abby said. But they continued doing it under the table, where they thought she couldn't see them.

"This sandpaper isn't working," Shea complained. Abby found him another piece, and when she returned to the table, Jackie was gone.

He popped up on the other side of the table

with the smaller pieces from the block set stuck to his head. "Hey, look at me, I'm a block-head."

Archie dissolved into giggles. Becca and Shea rolled their eyes. "Did you *glue* those to your head?" Abby asked.

"Yeah," Jackie replied happily. He danced around the kitchen with the blocks bobbing on his head. "Mr. Blockhead. I'm Mr. Blockhead," he sang. Even Becca and Shea had to laugh.

All Abby could think of was how she was going to get the glue out of Jackie's hair. (My friends and I privately refer to Jackie as "the Walking Disaster." Although he's very lovable, he's always into some kind of mess.)

Jackie tossed his head back and a block flew from his hair and hit Becca on the cheek. "Ow!" she shouted as her paint-stained hand flew to her face. "Ow! Ow! Ow!" She began to cry, spreading blue paint across her face.

"What's wrong?" Jessi asked, hurrying into the kitchen with Squirt toddling behind her. Then, "Oh!" she cried as she tripped over another of Jackie's blocks and banged into the table. She moaned as she rubbed her elbow. Squirt began to cry.

Jessi recovered enough to clean Becca up and put a cold cloth on her cheek. Then she soothed Squirt.

Abby brought Jackie to the sink and began pulling the blocks from his hair. "Ouch, that hurts," he complained.

"Well, who told you to put glue in your hair?" she replied. She stuck his head under the tap and poured dishwashing soap on it to scrub his hair clean. As she towel-dried it with a spattered dishcloth, she surveyed the kitchen. There was so much paint spattered around, she told me later it reminded her of a piece of modern art she'd seen in a museum once.

Art or not, she was sure Mrs. Rodowsky wouldn't appreciate it. "We better clean up this place," she said to Jessi.

By the time Mrs. Rodowsky returned, the kitchen was clean and the kids were watching TV. But Jessi and Abby decided that toy repair was something that the BSC members should do on their own.

CHAPTER 10

On Sunday morning, I once again made my way to the mall to report as an elf. It's funny how fast something becomes routine. In just one week, I'd discovered the fastest way to get to the employees' lounge. (Cut through Lear's men's department and use the elevator hidden behind the overcoat section, then take the fire-escape hall to a door leading behind the food court, then out again to the lounge.)

This Sunday I was already in my elf costume when Angela arrived. She looked pale and her hair was disheveled, almost as though she hadn't slept. "Hi, are you okay?" I asked.

She shook her red curls self-consciously. "Why? Do I look terrible?"

"No, just tired or something."

Angela nodded as she opened the bag containing her elf costume. "I hardly slept at all last night."

"How come?" I asked.

She turned away from me while she pulled off her stack-heeled boots. "Someone was making a lot of noise outside."

I wrinkled my forehead, not understanding. "Who was making noise?"

Shrugging, she looked up at me. "Who knows, who cares?" She shot me a forced smile. "Can you believe this is our last week?"

"No, it's going fast," I admitted. "Are you doing anything special for Christmas or whatever you celebrate?"

"Christmas," she said. "My family always celebrated Christmas so I guess that's my holiday. What am I doing? Nothing."

"Nothing? You mean nothing unusual, right?"

She laughed bitterly. "No, I mean nothing."

"Your family doesn't do anything for Christmas?"

She pulled up her striped tights before she spoke. "I don't know what they'll be doing," she finally replied with a sob. "I don't live with them anymore."

"Where do you live?" I asked, suddenly very concerned about her.

"The women's shelter in Stoneybrook."

I stood there with my mouth slightly open. My brain wouldn't form a thought. All I could do was absorb this unexpected information.

Angela smiled at me but her eyes were pools of tears. "What's it like?" She asked the question for me. "No fun. It's not like anyone is especially happy to be there. We don't have group sing-alongs or anything like that."

I smiled grimly. "I didn't think so. Why are you there?"

"It's only temporary," she replied. "My parents kicked me out."

I was shocked all over again. "What for?"

"Just for being me," she answered with a bitter laugh. "They don't like my clothes, or my makeup, or the way I choose to live my life. I think they figured that if they threw me out, I'd come back and do things their way. I can't, though."

"What's their way?" I asked.

"The respected ancient practice," she said, speaking as though she were some kind of guru. "All you have to do is be friends with *only* white middle-class kids, shop at *only* the *right* snooty stores, and think country club activities are the height of human civilization, and you too can live the Way of the Snob. That's what my parents believe, but it's not what I believe, and I can't live that way."

"I don't think I could either," I said thoughtfully.

"Yeah, well, I was constantly embarrassing

Mom and Dad just by my existence. There's not much room for individuality in their world."

"That's horrible. How can you stand being at the shelter, though?"

"Well . . . it isn't where I want to be. That's why I'm working so many hours here. So I can earn enough money to leave the shelter. I have friends in California who all rent a big house together on the beach. They said I can come live with them, but I need the dough to go. I almost have it."

"That's terrific," I said. "What about Christmas, though?"

"What about it?"

"How will you spend it?"

"I'll take a walk or something," she said with a shrug.

The lounge door swung open and Ms. Cerasi stepped in. "Why aren't you girls dressed?" she cried. "Your shift starts in two minutes."

"Sorry." I pulled off my sneakers hurriedly. "I didn't realize. We were talking."

Ms. Cerasi clapped her hands sharply. "Let's go," she said, then left.

"I could really get to dislike her a lot," Angela said, pulling on her pointed elf slippers.

"It's only another week," I reminded her as I struggled into my costume.

Angela was about to pull on her head mask,

but she stopped and propped it on the table. "In a way, I hate for this to end. At least now I wake up each day and know what I'll be doing. After this job ends, anything could happen."

"Good things will happen," I said, hoping I sounded confident. "You'll see."

Angela patted my arm. "You're a good friend. Thanks."

I nodded. "Okay, now let's get happy. It's elf time!"

We stuck our heads into our masks. Then we turned toward the door at the same moment, bumped into each other, and bounced back. That cracked us both up and broke our gloomy mood.

We headed out into the mall, weaving through the crowd and waving to the kids who shouted at us. And, although I danced around, played with kids, and gave out candy canes for the rest of the day, I couldn't get Angela's story out of my mind.

She wasn't much older than my friends and me. I couldn't imagine any of us trying to live on our own in just four years. Sure, maybe we'd go away to college, but that was *five* years from now. Most of us would be eighteen then. Besides, living at college isn't the same as being completely on your own.

I thought of her walking around by herself

on Christmas. It made me want to cry. In fact, once while I watched her comfort a sobbing toddler, I did shed a few quiet tears for her behind my mask.

Sometimes life seems to be no fair at all. And it should be fair, at *least* on Christmas Day.

CHAPTER 11

It wasn't until the last bell rang at school on Tuesday that I realized what a big scheduling conflict I was facing. All during our BSC meeting the day before, I had been looking at it in the record book, but I didn't make the connection. Maybe that's what being continually exhausted does to your brain.

I don't know why it popped into my head just as I was pulling my costume bag from my locker, but thank goodness it did.

Last month, Mrs. Bruno, Logan's mother, had hired me to baby-sit for Logan's five-year-old brother, Hunter, and his nine-year-old sister, Kerry. Normally, Logan would have helped her out, but he's on the volleyball team and he already knew he'd have a big pregame practice that day.

Suddenly, as I stood in front of my locker, I could recall Mrs. Bruno's every word. "I'm booking you early, Mary Anne, because I know how busy the holidays are for the BSC. Every year I take one day off from work and do all my holiday shopping in one sweep. That's what I'll be doing."

The problem was, I was supposed to work after school. I couldn't let her down, though. I ran to the lobby and phoned home. Luckily, Dawn answered. "It's me," I said breathlessly. "You have to do me a big favor. I'm supposed to sit for the Brunos today at four, but I can't make it. Could you cover for me?"

"Why can't you go?" she asked.

"Uh . . . uh . . . the fund-raiser. I promised to go to the mall to hand out flyers advertising it."

"Couldn't you do that another time?"

"If you can't cover for me, just say so," I snapped.

"No, I can do it," she replied, sounding offended. "I was just wrapping gifts but it can wait."

I thanked her and hung up. Racing out the door and down the school steps, I ran to the bus stop. I arrived in time to see a bus pull away. The phone call had put me behind schedule and I'd have to wait a full fifteen minutes for the next bus to come.

While I stood there, anxious about being late, I realized the temperature had dropped since earlier that afternoon. The sky was blanketed with heavy white clouds. It was what Dad calls a snow sky.

With a shiver, I thought of Angela. Was it warm enough at the shelter? Did she have heavy enough clothing with her? What were the blankets like there? I just couldn't imagine.

The bus finally arrived. It seemed to crawl, stopping at every single traffic light along the way. Amazingly, though, it arrived at the mall with a full two minutes for me to jump into my costume and get to Winter World.

I flew through the mall and up to the lounge, pulling open my bag as I burst through the door. Angela was there in her costume, except for her mask. She was on the pay phone by the door. "They won't accept the charges?" I heard her murmur, sounding crushed.

For a moment, I stopped my frantic dressing and looked at her as she hung up. Again, she answered my question before I asked it. "I thought I'd be mature and propose meeting my parents on Christmas so we could spend the day together and maybe talk," she explained. "But they won't accept my collect call."

"I have change," I offered, turning toward my bag for it.

"Forget it," Angela said. "They can afford the call, believe me. They don't want to talk to me, that's all."

"I'm sorry," I said, seeing the hurt on her face.

"Thanks. You better finish dressing or Ms. Cerasi will put you in elf prison or something equally terrible."

That afternoon, Winter World was hopping. The line of kids waiting to see Santa snaked around the platform. Marv was a terrific Santa, so cheerful and patient with the kids. One of them tried to pull his beard to prove to his little brother that Santa was a fake. The kid almost fell over when Marv's beard refused to budge. And you should have seen the little brother. His face lit up with joy.

The kids waiting in line were either fidgety or nervous, so I danced up and down the line giving out helium balloons and candy canes, trying to keep everyone happy. The kids cheered up whenever I came by.

And then, suddenly, my dancing screeched to a halt. Standing in line, only a few feet away, were Logan, Dawn, Mrs. Bruno, Hunter, and Kerry.

Inside my mask I gaped in horror. What were they doing here?

They were close enough so that I could hear their conversation. "I'll leave you all to visit Santa while I shop," Mrs. Bruno said, stepping away from the group. "We'll meet in front of the theater three hours from now, after you've seen your movie." With a wave, she hurried off.

Obviously they'd decided to see Santa and a movie while Mrs. Bruno shopped. But what was Logan doing there?

"It was a lucky break they canceled practice," he said to Dawn. "I didn't know when I'd be able to shop for Mary Anne. I know exactly what I'm getting her, though."

I felt so exposed standing there right in front of them. I had to force myself to remember I was hidden behind my mask.

"Oh, elf! Elf!" Dawn began calling and waving to me. "Over here, please. Could you come here?"

I froze. Had she recognized me? Did she know it was me?

"Elf! Elf!" Hunter called. I had no choice but to go to them.

"Could we have a balloon and a candy cane, please?" Dawn spoke for Hunter. Usually, I talked to the kids in a little squeaky voice, but I didn't dare open my mouth now. I simply handed each of them a candy cane and gave balloons to Hunter and Kerry. (Kerry made a self-conscious face as if she felt babyish, but she took the balloon anyway.)

Then there was a horrible moment when I stood waiting for Logan or Dawn to say something to me. At such close range, they *had* to know it was me.

Didn't they?

I waited.

"Thanks, Mr. Elf," Dawn said with a smile, seeming to sense I was waiting for something.

I forced a wave and danced away. Of course, I was relieved. But I also felt oddly let down.

One night around Thanksgiving break, I stayed up late and watched an old black-and-white movie called *Our Town*. At the end of it, a ghost comes back and sees all the people she loves, but they can't see her. It gives her a painful, heartbreaking, lonely feeling.

Strangely, that was how I felt. After all, Logan and Dawn are two of the people who are most important to me. I can't think of anyone who knows me better than they do, except maybe Kristy. And they didn't know I was standing right next to them. I hated the feeling.

Kids called to me and I acted cheerful, handing them candy and balloons, dancing and waving. Inside, though, I felt uneasy and sad. From time to time, I glanced over at Angela. She was doing the same, acting funny and cheerful. Inside, though, I knew her heart was breaking.

The line inched forward and in about ten minutes Dawn, Logan, Kerry, and Hunter were the next in line. Kerry took Hunter to Santa. I don't think she still believes in Santa, but she pretended to for Hunter, which I thought was nice.

From behind me, I felt a tug on my tunic. I turned and looked down at Hunter. In an instant, I realized he'd run back to me while Dawn, Logan, and Kerry waited.

" 'Bye, Mary Anne," he said.

I drew in a short, startled breath. Then I knelt down to face him. "How did you know?"

He shrugged. "I could just tell."

"Did you have a good talk with Santa?" I asked.

He nodded. "You're lucky to be an elf."

"I know, it's fun," I told him. "Listen, Hunter, could this be our secret? I'd feel a little silly if everyone knew I was an elf."

He stared at for me a moment, as if what I'd just said made no sense to him. Then he nodded. "Okay, if you don't want me to tell anyone, I won't."

"Thanks," I said. "You'd better get back to Dawn and Logan and Kerry. Have fun at the movies."

"Thanks. 'Bye, Mary Anne."

I waved as he ran off.

Funny, but I felt so grateful to him for recognizing me that tears welled in my eyes. I had no choice but to let them fall down my cheeks, because you can't wipe your eyes when you're wearing an elf head.

CHAPTER 12

One thing I'm very proud of is that I've never — not ever! — made a mistake in the club record book. I haven't double-booked a sitting job or overlooked someone's conflicting appointments. Or if I have, I've caught the mistake before it was too late.

But I had nearly goofed with my sitting job for Kerry and Hunter, and at the meeting that Wednesday I nearly goofed again.

"Stacey, you can sit for the Newtons this weekend," I told her after Mrs. Newton called wanting a sitter for Jamie and Lucy.

"Okay," she agreed as she picked up the phone to return Mrs. Newton's call.

Feeling zonked from my crazy schedule, I stared vacantly at the record book on my lap. The words on the page seemed to waver in front of my weary eyes. I blinked hard, attempting to pull them back into focus.

"Hello, Mrs. Newton?" As I focused on the

words before me, I was vaguely aware of Stacey's voice. "I'm going to sit for —"

"Wait!" I shouted. At the last moment, I'd concentrated enough to spot something I'd overlooked. "Stacey," I said. "Aren't you supposed to see the Christmas Show at Radio City Music Hall with your father that day?"

"Oh my lord!" Stacey gasped. "You're right. I forgot." She excused herself, apologizing, and told Mrs. Newton she'd have to call back again. "Mary Anne!" she cried as she hung up.

"Sorry," I said. "Sorry."

My friends were staring at me with surprised expressions. "So I made a mistake!" I said.

"At least it proves you're human," Jessi offered.

"Of course I'm human."

Everyone grinned and relaxed, except for Dawn, who had decided to sit in on the meeting. She held me in a scrutinizing gaze. What was she thinking?

Had Hunter broken his word and told her he'd recognized me as an elf? But Dawn said nothing.

We were very busy for the rest of the meeting. (And I double-checked every job I scheduled, determined not to goof again.) In between calls, we discussed the final plans for Santa-Hanukkah-Kwanzaa Town.

Abby and Jessi had finished refurbishing most of the not-so-good toys. As Abby had planned, the infamous blocks would be used to set up towers for a knock-down ball game booth. The cloth dolls and animals had been washed and stitched. They'd be used to toss through a donated hula hoop we planned to hang. Working plastic toys had been cleaned up and would be dumped into a kiddie plastic pool, and kids would get to fish for them with specially made fishing poles fitted with clothes-hanger hooks.

Those were just some of the ideas. It was going to be loads of fun for the kids who attended. (And Kristy got the go-ahead to use the elementary school gym.)

After the meeting, Dawn and I headed home together, though we hardly spoke. Finally, I couldn't stand it another second. "Dawn, I have to talk to you about something," I began in a faltering voice.

"What?" she asked, stopping. The look in her blue eyes was wary. It was as though there were a huge hole in the ground between us that neither of us could cross. I had to try, though.

"Ever since you've come home, I feel you've been extremely distant," I began, not looking at her. Somehow it was easier that way. "It's like you don't want to be friends or sisters anymore."

The last part was hard to say. Even the very idea of it hurt. What if she told me I was right — that it was exactly how she *did* feel?

"Me?" she cried. "Me?"

I looked at her and nodded. "Yes, you."

"*You're* the one who's been acting that way."

"Me?" I was truly astonished.

"Yes! You've been avoiding me ever since I got here," she accused. "You're *never* around. You tell Mom and Richard that you're with the BSC at the mall, but I know for a fact that you're not. Mary Anne, something is going on with you but I haven't got the slightest idea what it could be."

"You're right, something is going on . . . but . . . but . . . I can't tell you," I said.

Dawn folded her arms and turned away from me. "You've never kept a secret from me before," she said in a low, hurt voice.

She was right about that too, but it wasn't my fault. "How can I confide in you when you don't even seem like the same Dawn?"

Her mouth fell open and she looked as if I'd just tossed cold water on her, but I wasn't going to back down. I felt what I felt. "It's true!" I insisted. "You act like you're some superior high school kid now and the rest of us are just twerpy middle school nerds."

"I do not!"

"Yes, you do."

"You don't know what I act like. You haven't been around to know anything about how I feel and what I'm thinking." She spoke fast and her face was becoming flushed with anger. "You're so busy with your secret life — whatever *that's* about — that you don't even know I'm here. I might as well have stayed in California."

I couldn't help myself. I began to cry. "Well, you don't know what *I've* been dealing with."

Softening, she put her hand on my arm. "Then tell me," she said gently. "Why are you shutting me out?"

"All right! I'll tell you," I cried, brushing away my tears. "I'm an elf!"

Dawn frowned. "What?"

"It's true. I'm an elf. I was standing right next to you at Winter World yesterday."

A bemused smile formed on Dawn's lips. "Are you kidding?"

"It's not funny," I said. Then I tearfully told her the entire story. "I'm so tired, Dawn," I said. "You can't imagine."

"And you didn't tell anyone?" she asked. "Not even Logan?"

"Especially not him. "It would have been too embarrassing."

Dawn put her arm around me and hugged me. "Mary Anne, I had no idea you were such a nut," she said.

"I'm not a nut," I protested indignantly, wiping my eyes.

"Sure you are. Why didn't you tell somebody?"

"It's embarrassing and I figured I could just handle it myself and no one had to know."

"Well, that's nutty. Your friends might have made some jokes but it's not *that* embarrassing. They could have helped you out. At least you'd have been able to talk about it. Look at the trouble your secrecy caused. I was holding back with you because I felt you were holding back with me — and you were."

"But so were you," I replied.

"I know," she said. "Things haven't been so easy for me either. I only realized it the other day, but being with the high school kids makes me feel sort of pressured. I've been so relaxed here since I came back that I finally noticed the difference. With the older kids you always feel like you have to act cool and not seem like a twerp. That's become a habit and I didn't even realize I was doing it."

"You *were* doing it," I said sullenly.

"I guess so," she admitted. "But I stopped once I relaxed after the first day or so. Only you weren't around to notice."

I laughed. It was all so silly! And I felt so happy that it had been a misunderstanding, instead of a giant rift between Dawn and me.

We started walking again. For the first time in days I felt light and happy. I apologized for not taking Dawn into my confidence, then told her about life as an elf. "It sounds like fun," she commented.

"Sometimes it is and sometimes it's not." I told her about the heat and heaviness of the mask, about Ms. Cerasi's watchful eye, about having to comfort the crying kids who were freaked out by Santa.

I told her too about Angela. "I think of her walking around alone on Christmas Day and I feel so terrible."

"Invite her to our house," Dawn suggested, as if the idea should have been obvious.

And it should have been. My brain was so worn out and muddled I hadn't thought of it, though. "What a great idea," I cried. "Do you think Dad and your mom would mind?"

"Why should they?"

She was right. "I can't wait to get home and ask them," I said, picking up my pace.

Luckily, when we arrived home both Dad and Sharon were in the living room on the couch, reading the greeting cards they'd received that day. Without mentioning my secret job, I told them I knew a girl who'd been kicked out of her home and that I'd like to invite her for Christmas. "She's not a problem kid or anything," I explained. "Her parents just don't understand her."

"I don't know," Dad said. "There must be some reason her parents are unhappy with her. I'm not sure I want you associating with someone who can't get along in her own home."

"Mary Anne and I really want to do this," Dawn said. "Don't you think it's the right thing? I mean it's Christmas, after all."

"Richard," Sharon began, "do you remember how my parents felt about you when you were young? They sent me all the way to California just to get me away from you."

Dad grew slightly red at the temples. "Yes . . . well . . . in that case, they happened to be . . . misguided."

"Angela's parents are . . . *misguided* too," I said.

"It can't hurt to be kind to someone with nowhere to go on Christmas," Sharon said. She held out a greeting card to him that read: PEACE ON EARTH AND GOOD WILL TO ALL.

"Oh, all right. It *is* Christmas," Dad said, with a smile. "Invite your friend, Mary Anne."

"Yesss!" I cried, throwing my arms around him. "Thank you. I feel so much better about everything now!"

In fact, I felt wonderful!

Angela wouldn't spend a lonely Christmas. I couldn't wait to get to work tomorrow and tell her.

But more than anything, I was happy I'd told Dawn the truth. I had my sister back, and that felt so good I couldn't stop smiling.

CHAPTER 13

Thursday

When I first thought up the idea for the BSC I just figured it would be a smart way to earn money. But it's become much more than that. I was amazed by the way Santa-Hanukkah-Kwanzaa Town turned out.

On the day before Christmas Eve — while I was putting in my final shift as an elf — the BSC members busily set up for Santa-Hanukkah-Kwanzaa Town. I'd promised to help out the minute I could get to the elementary school. (I'd told a small lie and admitted I'd taken a part-time job at the mall, only I said I was working in the office.)

As you might imagine, Kristy was in hyper-drive mode, determined to make everything perfect by the time people entered the gym. While everyone else was setting up their booths, she raced around, a one-girl decorating committee.

She tacked up tissue-paper wreaths she'd made with her stepsister and stepbrother. Over the doorway she looped paper chains that she'd made with the Barrett-DeWitt kids one afternoon.

She was surprised when her stepdad and her mother showed up early, carrying a big Christmas tree between them. "We wanted to donate this," Watson said, propping up the tree in a stand he'd bought. "We have a box of ornaments in the car. Your mom and I will put them up."

"No, let the kids do it when they get here," Kristy suggested, always thinking. "They like doing that."

106

At exactly four o'clock, the moment we'd said we'd open, people began to arrive. Soon the booths were bustling. Jessi scurried back and forth between her two booths. One gave out information about Kwanzaa and sold raffle tickets to win a decorated basket of fruit, vegetables, cheese, and crackers. The basket had been assembled from donated items. It represented the aspect of Kwanzaa that celebrates the harvest. We also put Kwanzaa candles in the basket to go with the lighting of the kinara, a Kwanzaa tradition.

Jessi's second booth was the cloth-doll throw. Mallory was next to her with the block knock-down. She also ran the car race (a last-minute idea), at which kids tried to push some of the donated toy cars into a long cardboard tube and out the other end first to win a prize.

Claudia ran the food concession. Her sister, Janine, offered to help her. They dished out the chili and ziti we'd prepared. Buckets of ice kept the sodas cold.

Shannon Kilbourne and her younger sisters, Tiffany and Maria, ran a ring-toss game with a set they brought from home. Logan's game consisted of throwing a football through a tire.

Abby enlisted Anna to play her violin. Anna, in turn, asked some of the kids from the orchestra at school to join her, so there was live holiday music.

In celebration of Hanukkah, Abby conducted a dreidel craft table, where kids made dreidels from clay.

Kristy and Stacey ran around and helped wherever they were needed. Stacey was in charge of money (of course). She ran from booth to booth collecting it. She also assisted kids with placing ornaments on the tree.

Kristy set up a toy-donation box to collect the unwrapped new toys. Later she told me that for her this was the most surprising, inspiring part of the fair. Practically every person who came brought one or more new toys. Her donation box filled up so quickly that she had to run to the cafeteria for another box. "Wow! Everyone is being so generous," she commented to Stacey. "Maybe they can have a party with the money we're earning since I don't think they'll need to spend it on toys."

"Here comes Dr. Johanssen," Stacey pointed out as she spotted Charlotte and her mother crossing the gym toward her. "Wait until they see this."

Dr. Johanssen was truly impressed. "I wonder if we could send some of these new toys to the homeless shelter. Believe it or not, we have more than we need," she said.

Claudia hurried to them, looking excited. "The guy who owns Pizza Express was just here with his kids. He told me he's going to send a delivery of fifteen pies for us to sell."

"Awesome!" Kristy cried. She told me she felt so overwhelmed by everyone's generosity.

"I guess sometimes people just need a push in the right direction," she said to Stacey.

Stacey grinned at her. "Well, leave it to you, Santa's helper," she said. "You'd have made a great head elf."

Kristy beamed and gazed around. Then, noticing that the tree was decorated, except for the star, she hurried off to find a ladder.

CHAPTER 14

The mall was jam-packed that Thursday afternoon, but Winter World was oddly quiet. "I guess all the kids have already seen Santa," Marv surmised as he stood up from his throne and stretched. Every now and then someone would trickle in for a visit. Not often, though.

By the time I'd arrived at the lounge that afternoon, Angela was already at Winter World. I was so eager to invite her for Christmas that I asked her about it as soon as I stepped onto the Winter World platform.

It was odd. At a moment like that you look for someone's expression. Is she pleased? Surprised? All I could see was a grinning elf mask in front of me. Adding to my suspense was the fact that Angela didn't reply.

"It'll be fun," I coaxed. "My family is nice. You'll like them."

Then I heard sniffing from behind Angela's mask. "Are you crying?" I asked.

Her head bobbed up and down.

"Did something happen?"

She stepped closer so that our masks clunked lightly against each other. "No. I'd love to come. No one has done anything this nice for me in awhile, that's all."

What could it possibly be like to be so alone?

Ms. Cerasi approached us and I expected her to scold us for standing around chatting. Instead, she handed us each an envelope. "Here's your last pay," she said. "You girls can leave now if you like."

"I was scheduled to work tomorrow," Angela protested.

"Sorry, we won't be needing you. It's slower than we anticipated." I knew Angela was counting on that money, but there was nothing she could do about it.

Ms. Cerasi, chilly to the end, didn't say good-bye, or good luck, thanks, or even happy holidays. She simply turned and walked away. "And so we say a fond farewell to the Ice Queen of Winter World," Angela joked as Ms. Cerasi departed.

Marv said good-bye warmly, though, and so did the women who took the pictures. Then Angela and I bopped upstairs and yanked off our elf heads for the last time. "You know, now that it's over, I'm going to miss this goofy costume," I said sincerely.

Angela kissed her mask on its wide forehead. "Me too," she agreed. "Exploring the elf side of my personality has been very interesting."

As we changed out of our elf suits, I invited her to join me at Santa-Hanukkah-Kwanzaa Town. She declined, saying she had something to do at the shelter. "Okay. Come to my house as soon as you can tomorrow." I wrote down my address and gave her directions to Burnt Hill Road. "You can stay over tomorrow night so that you'll be there Christmas morning."

"That sounds great," she said warmly. "Thank you so much, Mary Anne."

I was happy Ms. Cerasi had let us off early since I wanted to hurry to the school gym. But after I'd dressed and Angela was gone, I realized I didn't have a gift for Angela. I didn't want her to watch my family exchange gifts without getting any herself.

As I rode down the escalator I wondered what a person on her own could really use. She was on her way to California, so she didn't need warm clothing. What, then? I tried to imagine myself in her situation. What would I most want?

I noticed a phone store that had opened in a formerly empty space just for the holiday season. Suddenly inspired, I ran inside and bought a phone card equal to twenty dollars worth of long-distance calls.

I'd decided that what I'd want most would be a connection to the people I cared about. I assumed it was what Angela wanted most too. A phone card might at least help.

By the time I arrived at Santa-Hanukkah-Kwanzaa Town, it was after six, and things were beginning to wind down.

Janine had gone home, so I sat with Claudia at the food booth. It was fortunate that Pizza Express had sent the fifteen pies or she'd have run out of food an hour earlier. "Mary Anne," she said casually as she popped open a soda. "Is everything all right with you?"

"Why do you ask?" I replied.

"You seem . . . different. I don't know. I'm worried about you."

It was time to be honest. I don't know why I hadn't been truthful all along. I told her about my job.

"Wow! That's a relief," she said. "I thought something terrible was happening. You looked so tired and faraway. Everyone's been concerned."

I felt happy. Despite wearing a mask and keeping a secret, I hadn't been invisible to my friends, not for a moment. They knew me and they cared.

Looking across the gym, I made eye contact

with Logan, who was still running his football toss. I pushed my chair back. "I want to tell Logan before he hears it from anyone else," I said to Claudia.

"You haven't even told him?" she asked.

"No, and I think he deserves an explanation."

CHAPTER 15

Logan was pleased that I'd finally been honest with him. Like my friends, he'd been concerned about me. "Not telling me was dumb," he said. "Sure, I'd have teased you, but you can tell me anything. You should know that."

That night I made the hardest confession of all. I found Dad and Sharon having tea in the kitchen and I sat down with them. "The good news is I'll be able to pay your credit card bill when it comes in," I said, after I'd told my story.

"And the bad news is that you lied to us," Dad said.

"I'm sorry," I replied sincerely. I was truly sorry I'd lied to any of the people I love. It was something I'd try never to do again.

"It's Christmas," Sharon said to Dad. "And the job is finished, and nothing bad came of it. Why don't we forget it for this once? If Mary Anne hadn't told us, we'd have never known."

Dad's face remained unreadable. A terrible quiet hung in the air while I waited for his response.

"This once," he agreed finally. "But the next time I learn you've done something behind my back, I won't let you off so easily."

"There won't be a next time," I assured him.

The next day was Christmas Eve. I awoke filled with holiday spirit.

Angela arrived at noon. Everyone else was out doing last-minute shopping, so I was alone waiting for her. "Don't worry," she said as she dragged a large suitcase through the front door. "I'm not moving in. I've earned enough for a plane ticket. After I leave here tomorrow, I'm headed for the airport."

"Great!" I cried. Then my smile faded. "Except, I won't see you anymore."

"I'll write," she promised. "The phone gets expensive."

I ran to the tree and pulled out an envelope with a bow on it, in which I'd put her phone card. "I just can't wait to give you this."

"I don't have anything for you," Angela said. "I didn't have the money. I'd have *liked* to get you something."

"Don't worry about it. Open the envelope," I said.

Her face lit up when she saw the phone card and she threw her arms around me. "Mary

Anne, this is so thoughtful. It's the most perfect gift."

She used the card then to phone her parents (this time *not* collect). "I wanted to say merry Christmas," I heard her say. And then, "That's not my fault, Mom. The other day I tried to call but —"

In a minute Angela sat down next to me in the living room. "My mom hung up on me," she reported, looking crushed.

"Call someone who'll be glad to hear from you," I suggested. I could never imagine Dad or Sharon hanging up on me, no matter what.

"My friends in California," she said, brightening. She checked her watch. "It's nine there. They'll be awake." Using her new card once again, she phoned them. "Yes, yes, I'm finally coming," she reported happily. I could tell from the rest of the conversation that this news was received with a lot of enthusiasm.

As Angela spoke on the phone, Dawn, Jeff, and Sharon returned. Dawn whispered in my ear, "We bought some gifts for Angela. We didn't want her to feel left out."

"Thank you," I whispered back.

Sharon hurried in with shopping bags, which she whisked upstairs for wrapping. Jeff turned on the TV. *It's a Wonderful Life* was playing. "Don't change it," I said. "I love this movie."

Angela hurried out of the kitchen, seeming very happy. "Hi," she greeted Dawn. "You must be the sister from California."

"And I guess you're Angela." Almost instantly they began talking enthusiastically about California. My attention wandered to the movie. It was the last scene, in which all of George Bailey's friends come through to replace the money his uncle misplaced. I started to tear up with happiness, as I always do at the end of this movie.

"Hey, is that *It's a Wonderful Life*?" Angela asked.

"Yes," I replied. "It sure is." That was exactly how I felt too. I have a wonderful life.

Dear Reader,

In *The Secret Life of Mary Anne Spier*, Mary Anne takes on the most embarrassing job of her life in order to earn money for holiday gifts for her friends and family. When I was younger, like Mary Anne I often needed to earn money to buy gifts for my family and friends. One memorable summer, when I was about nine, I suddenly realized that my parents' anniversary was just two weeks away and I didn't have enough money to buy them a present. So I talked my friend Beth into holding a backyard carnival with me. The money that I earned at the carnival was spent on a gift for my parents. But what a lot of work: Beth and I had to plan an entire carnival, borrow money from our parents to buy the materials we needed, and plan, announce, and run the carnival. All of this netted me seven dollars, but I was thrilled. I went to Woolworth's and bought them a set of orange juice glasses. Not as lavish as the gifts Mary Anne bought for her friends, but at least I didn't have to dress up as an elf!

Happy reading,

Ann M. Martin

Ann M. Martin

About the Author

ANN MATTHEWS MARTIN was born on August 12, 1955. She grew up in Princeton, NJ, with her parents and her younger sister, Jane.

Although Ann used to be a teacher and then an editor of children's books, she's now a full-time writer. She gets ideas for her books from many different places. Some are based on personal experiences. Others are based on childhood memories and feelings. Many are written about contemporary problems or events.

All of Ann's characters, even the members of the Baby-sitters Club, are made up. (So is Stoneybrook.) But many of her characters are based on real people. Sometimes Ann names her characters after people she knows, other times she chooses names she likes.

In addition to the Baby-sitters Club books, Ann Martin has written many other books for children. Her favorite is *Ten Kids, No Pets* because she loves big families and she loves animals. Her favorite Baby-sitters Club book is *Kristy's Big Day*. (By the way, Kristy is her favorite baby-sitter!)

Ann M. Martin now lives in New York with her cats, Gussie and Woody. Her hobbies are reading, sewing, and needlework — especially making clothes for children.

Notebook Pages

This Baby-sitters Club book belongs to _____.

I am _____ years old and in the _____

grade.

The name of my school is _____.

I got this BSC book from _____.

I started reading it on _____ and

finished reading it on _____.

The place where I read most of this book is _____.

My favorite part was when _____.

If I could change anything in the story, it might be the part when

_____.

My favorite character in the Baby-sitters Club is _____.

The BSC member I am most like is _____

because _____.

If I could write a Baby-sitters Club book it would be about _____

_____.

#114 The Secret Life of Mary Anne Spier

In *The Secret Life of Mary Anne Spier*, Mary Anne needs to [make] some quick money in order to pay off her credit card bill. [She] spent too much money on presents! Choosing presents can be very hard. The easiest person for me to buy a present for is _____ .

The hardest person to buy a present for is _____ _____ . The next time I buy my best friend a present, I am going to buy her/him a _____ _____ . One present I really want is _____ _____ . The best present I ever received was when _____ _____ gave me _____ _____ . The best present I ever gave was a _____ _____ for _____ _____ . It is always fun for Mary Anne to shop for her BSC friends. If I were shopping for the BSC members, I would buy _____ for Kristy, _____ _____ for Claudia, _____ for Mary Anne, _____ _____ for Stacey, _____ for Mallory, _____ for Jessi, and _____ _____ for Abby. Hopefully I wouldn't have to work as an elf to afford all these presents!

MARY ANNE'S

Party girl -- age 4

Sitting for the Pikes is always an adventure.

Sitting for Andrea and Jenny Prezzioso -- a quiet moment.

SCRAPBOOK

*Logan and me.
Summer luv at Sea City.*

*My family...
Jeff, Dad and Sharon.
Dawn and me. And Tigger.*

Read all the books
about **Mary Anne**
in the Baby-sitters Club series
by Ann M. Martin

Portrait Collection:

Look for #115

JESSI'S BIG BREAK

"Jessica," Mama said. "You'll be alone in a strange city —"

"It's not strange," I protested. "I've been there lots of times. And I won't be alone either. I'll be in class all day and with Michael and Marian at night —"

"Michael and Marian?" Daddy asked. "Have you called them?"

"Well, no, not yet," I replied. "But I *could* stay with them."

"They're a young couple," Aunt Cecelia said. "They have their busy-busy lives, never home, working into the night on goodness knows what, never even have enough time to talk to their own mother — how could they possibly handle you?"

"Call and ask!" I pleaded.

"I could try, but I always get their answering machine," Aunt Cecelia said. "Answering machines makes me very uncomfortable."

"Stay with us," said Becca.

"Dess-see," said Squirt.

I looked hopefully at my mom and dad.

Mama took my hand. "Look, your father and I have been discussing this possibility since your audition. It's a major thing for an eleven-year-old girl to do — living in the big city, not knowing anyone . . ."

My stomach was sinking.

"But we knew that if we said no," Daddy continued, "we would regret it the rest of our lives."

"So . . . I can go?"

Daddy stood up and kissed me on the forehead. "Let me call Michael's answering machine right now. Maybe if he hears that it's not his meddling mom on the phone, he'll pick up."

"Well, I *never* —" Aunt Cecelia huffed.

"Lucky!" Becca said, stomping out of the room.

"Dutty!" Squirt echoed.

Me? I don't remember what I said. I was floating somewhere near the ceiling.

I have never been so happy in all my life.

Collect them all!

☐ MG43388-1	#1	Kristy's Great Idea	$3.50
☐ MG43387-3	#10	Logan Likes Mary Anne!	$3.99
☐ MG43717-8	#15	Little Miss Stoneybrook...and Dawn	$3.50
☐ MG43722-4	#20	Kristy and the Walking Disaster	$3.50
☐ MG43347-4	#25	Mary Anne and the Search for Tigger	$3.50
☐ MG42498-X	#30	Mary Anne and the Great Romance	$3.50
☐ MG42508-0	#35	Stacey and the Mystery of Stoneybrook	$3.50
☐ MG44082-9	#40	Claudia and the Middle School Mystery	$3.25
☐ MG43574-4	#45	Kristy and the Baby Parade	$3.50
☐ MG44969-9	#50	Dawn's Big Date	$3.50
☐ MG44968-0	#51	Stacey's Ex-Best Friend	$3.50
☐ MG44966-4	#52	Mary Anne + 2 Many Babies	$3.50
☐ MG44967-2	#53	Kristy for President	$3.25
☐ MG44965-6	#54	Mallory and the Dream Horse	$3.25
☐ MG44964-8	#55	Jessi's Gold Medal	$3.25
☐ MG45657-1	#56	Keep Out, Claudia!	$3.50
☐ MG45658-X	#57	Dawn Saves the Planet	$3.50
☐ MG45659-8	#58	Stacey's Choice	$3.50
☐ MG45660-1	#59	Mallory Hates Boys (and Gym)	$3.50
☐ MG45662-8	#60	Mary Anne's Makeover	$3.50
☐ MG45663-6	#61	Jessi and the Awful Secret	$3.50
☐ MG45664-4	#62	Kristy and the Worst Kid Ever	$3.50
☐ MG45665-2	#63	Claudia's Freind Friend	$3.50
☐ MG45666-0	#64	Dawn's Family Feud	$3.50
☐ MG45667-9	#65	Stacey's Big Crush	$3.50
☐ MG47004-3	#66	Maid Mary Anne	$3.50
☐ MG47005-1	#67	Dawn's Big Move	$3.50
☐ MG47006-X	#68	Jessi and the Bad Baby-sitter	$3.50
☐ MG47007-8	#69	Get Well Soon, Mallory!	$3.50
☐ MG47008-6	#70	Stacey and the Cheerleaders	$3.50
☐ MG47009-4	#71	Claudia and the Perfect Boy	$3.99
☐ MG47010-8	#72	Dawn and the We ♥ Kids Club	$3.99
☐ MG47011-6	#73	Mary Anne and Miss Priss	$3.99
☐ MG47012-4	#74	Kristy and the Copycat	$3.99
☐ MG47013-2	#75	Jessi's Horrible Prank	$3.50
☐ MG47014-0	#76	Stacey's Lie	$3.50
☐ MG48221-1	#77	Dawn and Whitney, Friends Forever	$3.99
☐ MG48222-X	#78	Claudia and Crazy Peaches	$3.50
☐ MG48223-8	#79	Mary Anne Breaks the Rules	$3.50
☐ MG48224-6	#80	Mallory Pike, #1 Fan	$3.99
☐ MG48225-4	#81	Kristy and Mr. Mom	$3.50
☐ MG48226-2	#82	Jessi and the Troublemaker	$3.99
☐ MG48235-1	#83	Stacey vs. the BSC	$3.50
☐ MG48228-9	#84	Dawn and the School Spirit War	$3.50
☐ MG48236-X	#85	Claudi Kishi, Live from WSTO	$3.50
☐ MG48227-0	#86	Mary Anne and Camp BSC	$3.50
☐ MG48237-8	#87	Stacey and the Bad Girls	$3.50
☐ MG22872-2	#88	Farewell, Dawn	$3.50

More titles... ➡

❏ MG22873-0	#89	Kristy and the Dirty Diapers	$3.50
❏ MG22874-9	#90	Welcome to the BSC, Abby	$3.99
❏ MG22875-1	#91	Claudia and the First Thanksgiving	$3.50
❏ MG22876-5	#92	Mallory's Christmas Wish	$3.50
❏ MG22877-3	#93	Mary Anne and the Memory Garden	$3.99
❏ MG22878-1	#94	Stacey McGill, Super Sitter	$3.99
❏ MG22879-X	#95	Kristy + Bart = ?	$3.99
❏ MG22880-3	#96	Abby's Lucky Thirteen	$3.99
❏ MG22881-1	#97	Claudia and the World's Cutest Baby	$3.99
❏ MG22882-X	#98	Dawn and Too Many Sitters	$3.99
❏ MG69205-4	#99	Stacey's Broken Heart	$3.99
❏ MG69206-2	#100	Kristy's Worst Idea	$3.99
❏ MG69207-0	#101	Claudia Kishi, Middle School Dropout	$3.99
❏ MG69208-9	#102	Mary Anne and the Little Princess	$3.99
❏ MG69209-7	#103	Happy Holidays, Jessi	$3.99
❏ MG69210-0	#104	Abby's Twin	$3.99
❏ MG69211-9	#105	Stacey the Math Whiz	$3.99
❏ MG69212-7	#106	Claudia, Queen of the Seventh Grade	$3.99
❏ MG69213-5	#107	Mind Your Own Business, Kristy!	$3.99
❏ MG69214-3	#108	Don't Give Up, Mallory	$3.99
❏ MG69215-1	#109	Mary Anne to the Rescue	$3.99
❏ MG05988-2	#110	Abby the Bad Sport	$3.99
❏ MG05989-0	#111	Stacey's Secret Friend	$3.99
❏ MG05990-4	#112	Kristy and the Sister War	$3.99
❏ MG45575-3		Logan's Story Special Edition Readers' Request	$3.25
❏ MG47118-X		Logan Bruno, Boy Baby-sitter Special Edition Readers' Request	$3.50
❏ MG47756-0		Shannon's Story Special Edition	$3.50
❏ MG47686-6		The Baby-sitters Club Guide to Baby-sitting	$3.25
❏ MG47314-X		The Baby-sitters Club Trivia and Puzzle Fun Book	$2.50
❏ MG48400-1		BSC Portrait Collection: Claudia's Book	$3.50
❏ MG22864-1		BSC Portrait Collection: Dawn's Book	$3.50
❏ MG69181-3		BSC Portrait Collection: Kristy's Book	$3.99
❏ MG22865-X		BSC Portrait Collection: Mary Anne's Book	$3.99
❏ MG48399-4		BSC Portrait Collection: Stacey's Book	$3.50
❏ MG69182-1		BSC Portrait Collection: Abby's Book	$3.99
❏ MG92713-2		The Complete Guide to The Baby-sitters Club	$4.95
❏ MG47151-1		The Baby-sitters Club Chain Letter	$14.95
❏ MG48295-5		The Baby-sitters Club Secret Santa	$14.95
❏ MG45074-3		The Baby-sitters Club Notebook	$2.50
❏ MG44783-1		The Baby-sitters Club Postcard Book	$4.95

Available wherever you buy books...or use this order form.

Scholastic Inc., P.O. Box 7502, Jefferson City, MO 65102

Please send me the books I have checked above. I am enclosing $_____
(please add $2.00 to cover shipping and handling). Send check or money order–
no cash or C.O.D.s please.

Name_____Birthdate_____

Address_____

City_____State/Zip_____

BSC5962

THE BABY-SITTERS CLUB®

by Ann M. Martin

Collect and read these exciting BSC Super Specials, Mysteries, and Super Mysteries along with your favorite Baby-sitters Club books!

BSC Super Specials

BSC Mysteries

More titles ➡

The Baby-sitters Club books continued...

Available wherever you buy books...or use this order form.
Scholastic Inc., P.O. Box 7502, Jefferson City, MO 65102-7502

Please send me the books I have checked above. I am enclosing $ _____
(please add $2.00 to cover shipping and handling). Send check or money order
— no cash or C.O.D.s please.

Name_____Birthdate_____

Address   _____

City_____State/Zip_____

Please allow four to six weeks for delivery. Offer good in the U.S. only. Sorry, mail orders are not available to residents of Canada. Prices subject to change.

BSCM497